North Murder Beach
A Jake Stellar Novel

By: Rodney Riesel

Copyright © 2014 Rodney Riesel

All rights reserved

Published by Island Holiday Publishing

East Greenbush, NY

ISBN: 978-0-9894877-6-4

Second Edition

Special thanks to:

Jamie Farrington

Pamela Guerriere

Kevin Cook

Cover Design by:

Connie Fitsik

To obtain more copies of this book friend me at

https://www.facebook.com/rodneyriesel

For Brenda

Kayleigh, Ethan,

&

Peyton

Chapter One

A morning run on the beach is always the best way to start the day. Well, maybe the second best way. We had started the day the *best* way and were now working on the *second* best.

It was a little after ten in the morning, a little late to start a run. It was already up around eighty degrees. The humidity was high for this time of the year and was making it a little difficult to take a deep breath. When I looked down I could feel the heat coming off of the pavement. My shirt was soaked through and I was wishing I hadn't lost my sun glasses the night before.

A good long run can sometimes get rid of a headache but this morning it was having the opposite effect. What had started out as a mere inconvenience was throbbing with every beat of my heart. As each step pounded the pavement I felt as though the front of my skull might explode sending hunks of gray matter, shards of skull, and blood into the street in front of me. *Wouldn't want to slip in it and twist my ankle.*

I looked to my running partner. She was a few steps ahead of me. She glanced back and smiled. I managed a little smile back at her.

Damn it, I thought. She was showing no signs of fatigue. I guess that's what being seven years younger and seventy pounds lighter can do for you. *I gotta lose some weight.* I wiped the sweat from my brow and slung it to the road. It returned almost instantly. I thought about taking my shirt off. *Negatory.* Not out here on the street where someone I might know may drive by and see my man tits flopping in the breeze. *I gotta hit the gym.*

We always start our runs on the street and end them on the sand. This morning we took Hillside Drive to Seventeenth, and then took a left on to South Ocean Boulevard. I looked over toward Molly Darcy's as we ran by.

We have to get over here for some of those wings," she said.

"Uh-huh," was about all I could get out. She had read my mind. Those whiskey wings are awesome.

"You OK?" she asked.

"Yeah," I lied. "Some pain in my left arm. A little pressure in my chest and the right side of my face is starting to sag."

She giggled. "Do you want to stop?"

"A little further," I gasped.

We got to Eleventh Avenue and ran down through the public access to the beach and turned back toward home.

We made it back to Twenty-First when I had had all I could take. I started walking.

I said, "That's it for me." I bent over and put my hands on my knees. The sweat dripped off my head, making tiny little craters in the damp sand.

She stopped running, too, but kept walking. I looked up and watched her walk toward the water, my hands still resting on my knee-caps, the sweat still stinging my eyes.

She looked good from behind. She always did. She was forty-one years old, but from behind she could easily pass for twenty-one. When I met her I thought she was the most beautiful woman I had ever seen. Seven years later, when we were married, I thought the same thing. After being married for thirteen years, nothing had changed. Her beauty still amazes me.

When Bree got to the edge of the water she bent down to untie her shoes. Bending over was a good look for her. She wore a pair of tight black running shorts that barely covered her butt cheeks, and when she bent over they didn't. She looked back at me. I was grinning.

"What?" she asked, forcing a frown. "Stop grinning like that."

"Stop bending over like that."

"You're a pig."

"I don't think you're supposed to call a cop a pig these days," I said. "At least not to his face. Anyway, I think only hippies said it."

Bree looked slightly annoyed, which only made her more attractive to me, as if that were really possible. "Thank you for the history lesson," she mocked.

She removed her shoes and socks; so did I. She faced the water, pushed up on her tip toes and stretched her arms up over her head. The muscles in her back and legs bulged. She was in great shape. Bree was muscular, but not too muscular. She was five foot three, had shoulder-length hair. This month it was brown with a little red mixed in. She had dark skin and dark brown eyes.

I took off my shirt and tucked it into my shorts. My muscles didn't show as well as Bree's. They were there, but at forty-seven they were now covered with a thin layer of fat. With my shirt on I appeared to be in much better shape. I was just glad at this age to still be sporting a full head of hair.

We walked along the beach at the edge of the water. The waves would come in and the water would rise to our ankles and recede. The sun was behind us now. It felt cooler by the water. I bent down filling my cupped hands with water and splashed it on my face and ran my fingers through my hair. My headache was disappearing. We held hands. We always held hands.

"How far did you want to walk?" she asked.

I shrugged. "I don't care. As far as you want."

"When do you have to be back to work?"

"The seventh."

It was the first day of my vacation. I had taken eight days off. I took about a week off every year at this time. It was a good time of the year to take a break. The spring bike rallies were over. The college kids were done with their spring breaks. Most families didn't book their vacations this close to bike week, so the next week was usually pretty slow.

I'm a cop, a detective with the North Myrtle Beach Police Department; violent crimes division. After graduating from the police academy in the Bronx I was assigned to the 48th Precinct, also in the Bronx. I was in a uniform for eight years before making detective, third grade and another six years to make it to detective first grade. Five years later I was burned out and looking for something at a little slower pace. North Myrtle Beach was just the right pace.

"Did you want to do anything, go anywhere?" Bree asked.

"I wouldn't mind starting every day of vacation like we did today."

"I'm guessing you're not talking about the run?"

"No, I'm not."

"I'm not doing that every day. Remember, I'm on vacation too."

"Your *vagina's* not on vacation." I replied.

"What's wrong with you?"

"You would be better off making a list of what's *not* wrong with me. It'd be a helluva lot shorter."

"You got that right," she whispered under her breath.

"Hey, I heard that." She *knew* I heard that. "When do you have to be back to work?"

"Not till the ninth."

Bree is a nurse, an RN. She spent fifteen years in the ER at Saint Barnabas, in the Bronx, before we moved here. That's where we met. I was in a uniform back then. I was five years on the job at the time. She was in her first year of nursing. She was twenty-one. I was twenty seven. I had brought in some kid that was whacked out on something. I don't remember what. Ecstasy, maybe. He had tried to rob a liquor store with one of those Rambo knives, you know, the kind with the compass on the handle, fishing hooks and water proof matches inside. Somehow he managed to stab himself four times without injuring anyone else in the liquor store. The ambulance came and transported him to St. Barnabas; I followed in my patrol car. Bree was working in the emergency room that night. I stared a hole into her in that form-fitting uniform, my brain already conjuring up naughty nurse-cop scenarios. She got the message and looked over at me. Our eyes met. She smiled. If there is such thing at love at first sight, that was it.

I got Bree's phone number from a friend of mine that also worked at the hospital. I called her a few days later. It took me that long to work up the nerve. We went on our first date that weekend, a seafood place. Bree ordered chicken, my first subtle clue to her rebellious streak. We saw a movie after dinner, *Under Siege*, with Steven Seagal as a kick-ass cook who saves the USS *Missouri* from terrorists. A good old-fashioned, balls-to-the wall, two-tubs-of-popcorn, manly-man, bullets-and-testosterone orgy. It wasn't her kind of movie, but she didn't complain. I promised to take her to a chick flick the next time.

"The ninth? What are you gonna do those two extra days without me?" I asked her.

"Those will be the only two days I get to rest."

"Thanks."

We walked all the way to the Twenty-Seventh Avenue access. As we made our way up the path I reached into my pocket and pulled out the three quarters wrapped in tissue I had brought to pay for the morning paper. I always wrapped the quarters so I didn't have to hear them jingle in my pocket. That's annoying. I walked over to the big blue metal box that contained the *Sun News*, put in my quarters, and pulled out the paper.

I rarely read the morning paper, but it was something I enjoyed doing on vacation. I rolled up the paper and smacked Bree on the ass with it when I caught up to her.

"You have issues, Jake."

"I never said I didn't."

We walked up Twenty-Seventh to Hillside, our street, and down two blocks to our house at the corner of Hillside and Twenty-Fifth.

Our house is one story; three bedrooms and two baths. The siding is beige stucco with white trim, and stone around the foundation. The roof is dark brown architectural shingles. We have a driveway off of Twenty-Fifth Avenue that leads to a two-stall garage, and a horseshoe driveway off of Hillside. There are three palm trees between the horseshoe driveway and the side walk. The house numbers are on the wall to the left of the door: 2502. Big brass jobs, turning a puke green with age. Above the numbers is a sign that reads, THE STELLARS.

Be it ever so humble, as they say.

Chapter Two

I sat at the kitchen table in my usual chair, the one that faced Hillside Drive. I like to look up from my paper and watch cars drive by or people walk by. I've always liked to watch people. It's not the cop in me, but rather the neighbor in me. I guess I'm just nosey. If I hear a lawn mower running I look out the window to see who is mowing their lawn. If I hear kids yelling I look out the window to see whose kids it is. It annoys the hell out of Bree until I remind her our neighbors probably do the same thing.

I was drinking a cup of coffee and reading the morning paper. Bree was in the shower. I had offered to join her, just to save water. You know, to help the environment. She declined. Obviously she cares nothing for the future of our planet. I don't think we had taken a shower together in at least five years. I better make a mental note to put in more effort on that.

I took a small sip of coffee and burned my upper lip. I winced. The coffee was coconut flavored. Call me a pussy, but I like flavored coffees. Right then we were working on a box of Wild Mountain Berry, as well as the box of coconut coffee. We had recently been given a Keurig coffee maker as a gift, a rather nice, expensive one at that. It was making coffee time much more enjoyable, but it made coffee a hell of a lot hotter than the old coffee maker. I rubbed my tongue against my upper lip to feel the temporary scar tissue. Burning your lip is almost as bad as biting it.

I had read most of the local stories. I had skimmed through the sports. The Yankees were in first place in the AL East, and Boston was in last place. Nice, but it was early in the year and I wouldn't be watching many games. The cable company didn't carry the YES network. *Bummer.*

I quickly scanned through the funnies only reading the ones that I read as a kid: *Hagar the Horrible, Garfield, B.C.*, oldies but goodies. I never really gave a shit about *Zits, Cul De Sac, or Pooch Cafe.* As far as I'm concerned each comic strip should only be allowed one talking dog. And too many modern strips trip over themselves trying to be hip and quirky. Screw that. Then I went back to the crossword puzzle. I picked up the pen I had laid on the table in anticipation of enjoying the crossword. I've always been pretty good at crossword puzzles, the ones at the *Sun News* level, of course. Not the *New York Times* or anything like that. As everyone who does crosswords knows, you don't have to be that bright to do them. You just have to do them often.

I was more than half way through the puzzle when Bree exited the bathroom and walked down the hallway to the kitchen. She was wearing nothing but a towel, two towels, actually. A brown one wrapped around her torso, and a beige one wrapped around her head. I watched her walk toward me. She looked at me and smiled.

"Let me see," I said, grinning.

She rolled her eyes, stopped, and opened the towel. She stood with the towel open for about ten seconds. "Good enough?" she asked, and then refastened it. She grinned, turned and walked toward the guest room. "You have issues," she said over her perfect shoulder.

I watched her walk away. Rituals and traditions are fun in a marriage, especially when they involve nudity.

"I like your hat," I called down the hall. "But I don't think it will go with the outfit." I returned to my crossword.

"Thanks," she hollered back.

"Anytime."

A few moments later I yelled to Bree in the other room. "Six letter word. Determine medical priority."

She immediately yelled back, "Triage."

"Thanks." I can always depend on her for the medical clues.

After fifteen minutes or so she walked back into the kitchen fully dressed. She was wearing denim shorts, the type that look like they were cut from long pants, frayed at the bottom, faux Daisy Dukes from Kohl's. The shorts had a couple of thread-bare holes in them, put there by some *whole in the pants* genius in some factory somewhere in a foreign country where college students are allowed to major in *pant holes*, for Chrissake. She had on a tight "Margaritaville" T-shirt; it was multi-colored and had a giant parrot on the front. She was wearing tan flip-flops. Turns out, the towel on her head would have matched the rest of her outfit, but I figured she wasn't leaving the house wearing it.

"Did you want to take a shower now?" she asked.

"Yeah. I'll jump in in a second."

I closed the paper and laid it on the table. I reread the front page headline to myself:

NORTH MYRTLE BEACH WOMAN SHOT DEAD IN HER HOME

"Why does the name Helen Gere sound familiar?" I asked.

Bree answered, "I don't know. It does sound familiar though. Why do you ask?"

"The paper says she was found dead in her home over on First Avenue last night." I immediately regretted bringing it up.

"That's horrible."

"She was sixty-eight years old," I said, hoping my tone didn't suggest that whoever Helen Gere was, she had lived long enough.

"Husband … children?" Bree asked.

"Doesn't say. Probably be more in tomorrow's paper."

I got up from my chair and made my way down the hall toward our bedroom. The master bath had been designated *my* bathroom long ago. I had always figured it was due to the fact that it was a lot smaller than the main bathroom, but I never asked. I had no vote in that election. The master bath had only a shower stall. I hadn't taken a bath in years. It also had only one small medicine chest over the sink. Plenty of room for a tooth brush, razor, and deodorant.

The other bathroom, Bree's Spa, as we called it, had a large whirlpool tub with a shower. There were several shelves in the shower, all filled with various types of shampoos, conditioners, treatments, moisturizing soaps, and body scrubs. Her "spa" also had several cabinets as well as a medicine chest. All of the cabinets were full. I've looked in the cabinets on several occasions, whether out of curiosity or out of her leaving a door open. I'm not quite sure what all of that stuff is, but I'm sure there is no way she uses all of it. I learned long ago that the question, "Why don't you throw away a bunch of that shit you don't use?" can cause quite a stir, and may even get a bottle of Wen shampoo thrown at one's head.

"Did you want me to make something for breakfast?" Bree asked, as I walked down the hall.

I turned back, "Well we could go out for breakfast."

She looked at the clock on the microwave. "It's already ten thirty. Do you want to go out for an early lunch in a little while instead?"

"Sounds good to me. You decide where while I'm in the shower."

*****

After I showered I went to, *my* closet, to pick out something to wear. My closet was so named around the same time as *my* bathroom. My closet was the closet in our bedroom. Bree's closet was the closet in one of the guest rooms. It was also all of the shelves I had put up in that guest room over the years to keep up with her ever-growing wardrobe, as well as the four closet rods I had also put up. Bree had a lot of clothes. I figured that she had one article of clothing she didn't wear per article of personal care product she didn't use. This brings me to another lesson I once learned. Never ask the question, "Why don't you throw away a bunch of that shit you don't ever wear?"

Chapter Three

I found Bree sitting by the pool at a small wrought iron table and chairs set we had purchased last year at a shop in the Market Commons. I pulled out the other chair and sat. She was reading the paper. A pen was lying on the table alongside a sweating as a glass of ice water. Her hair was still a little damp and she had it pulled back into a ponytail.

"Finished the crossword puzzle," she proudly announced.

"What was 'mountain goat'?" I asked.

"Ibex."

"How the hell did you know that?"

"I looked it up."

"That's cheating."

"What's the penalty?"

"Life … with me."

"I hope there's a possibility of parole."

"Only for *good* behavior, and I think this morning's *bad* behavior counts you out."

"Okay, okay no need to discuss this morning's activities."

"Sorry. Sometimes I like to recap the high lights."

"There were highlights?"

"I thought it was some of my best work."

Bree rolled her eyes. "I'm ready to go, are you?"

"Yut," I replied with a mock salute.

We got up from the table and made our way through the house to the garage. "My car or yours?" I asked.

"Yours. Mines on E."

"Of course it is." I glared at Bree. She tried not to make eye contact. She walked toward her car anyway, knowing full well this was her chance to get a free tank of gas.

"I can pump the gas," she said. "You just have to go in and pay."

"I'm not going to have you pump the gas while I go in and pay. What kind of man would do that? I would look like an idiot."

"Then what's the problem?"

I opened the door for Bree. "Like I said the last five hundred times, I hate going somewhere to eat with my hands smelling like gas."

"Sounds like someone should switch over to the super-absorbent pads," she said, climbing in. I shut the door.

"Did you decide where you wanted to eat?" I asked as we headed down Seventeenth Avenue. Bree shook her head no. I turned into the Circle K.

Bree said, "Grab some chips or something when you go in to pay."

"I wasn't going in to pay. I was going to use a credit card."

"And some dip," she added.

"Sure." I knew it was either get chips now or run out at nine-thirty tonight when she decided she was hungry for *some kind of snack.*

I put my money clip back in my pocket and headed in to pre-pay. I hate pre paying. Why don't they just hang up a sign that says, 'We don't trust any of you assholes, but please come on in and buy shit from us'? Besides, how do I know how much gas my car will hold this time? I usually just end up getting thirty bucks worth. I would hate to give them a fifty, and then my car only takes forty-eight. I would have to walk all the way back in and get my change. Maybe Bree is right. Maybe I better switch over to the super absorbent pads.

I waited in line behind a kid buying a grape soda and a small bag of Cool Ranch Doritos, and a very large black woman who was handing in winning scratch-offs. The kid was already drinking the soda he hadn't paid for yet. My mother never let me do that. She had me convinced that the moment I opened anything in the store that hadn't been paid for yet, that cops would burst through the door and a SWAT team would rappel from the ceiling. When I became a cop I learned that that rarely happened.

"Gimme a Bingo Night, and three Bronze Bucks, and two All The Marbles ... No wait."

Come on, lady, take your winnings and go. Don't give it all back to them, for Chrissake.

"...And two Big Bang Bucks. Um... I think that's it."

God, I hope so.

The kid with the soda looked back at me and rolled his eyes. He had a Mohawk haircut. I didn't think those were really popular anymore. His eyes were blue and he had light brown hair. Cute little bastard. He had on a tan golf shirt, Polo, tucked into his blue cargo shorts and he wore a belt. The boy was only about eight years old. His mother picked out those clothes this morning. She cared how he looked. He took another sip. I thought about drawing my revolver and asking him if he had paid for that yet, but decided against it. He turned around and stepped up to the counter, paid, and left. As he walked by me he looked up and smiled. I smiled back. I watched him as he walked out the door.

"Next."

The boy got on his bike and rode away.

"Next."

"Oh sorry," I muttered.

I gave my thirty bucks to the girl behind the counter and walked back to the car.

"Where's the chips?"

Crap.

After pumping my gas I walked back into the store.

The pencil-thin red-head, about sixteen, behind the counter watched me from behind her Coke bottle glasses.

She looked like Olive Oyl's homelier sister. "Forget something?"

"Chips."

After choosing corn chips, potato chips, ranch dip, salsa, and a can of nacho cheese, I walked back to the counter a second time, hoping that I had covered all of the snack bases. *No line this time. Thank God.*

As she rang me up she said, "Did you hear about Helen?"

I looked up from my money clip. The girl's eyes gleamed. She was practically frantic to gossip. "Helen who?"

"Helen Gere."

How do I know that name? I said nothing.

"Helen Gere! She works here… Nights." She held her hand about five feet off the floor. "About yay tall, gray hair."

It clicked. Sixty-eight, killed in her home, First Avenue. "Oh, yeah. I read that in the paper this morning. Didn't make the connection. Was she married?"

"No. Her husband died a few years back."

"Kids?" I asked.

"Two daughters. One up north somewhere and one in Wilmington."

"That's too bad." I paid and walked toward the door.

The kid obviously didn't want me to leave. "I never knew anybody that was murdered before," she said leadingly, but the door was already swinging closed behind me.

I did know Helen Gere. I saw her one or two nights a week for the last few years. I should have remembered her name. After all, about a year or so ago I questioned her about an attempted robbery here at this very same Circle K. Nothing much happened. A kid, seventeen years old, came in to rob the place. According to Helen, the kid tried the old "This is a stick-up" line. Just as the kid gets out the last word, in walks an armored truck driver on his lunch break. The kid takes one look at the guy's uniform and gun and almost knocks him down trying to get out of the door. We plastered the kid's picture from the surveillance camera all over the news. We got him two days later. Funny, I remembered all of that, but I didn't remember Helen's name.

I threw the bag in the back window and climbed into the car. I thought it best not to mention Helen Gere. Bree doesn't take things like that very well. Sympathy and empathy are her kryptonite.

"Did you decide where you want to eat?" I asked.

"No."

We pulled back on to Seventeen and waited at the stop light.

"Which way?" I asked.

"Left," she answered.

Chapter Four

For lunch, Bree had settled on Joe's Crab Shack at Barefoot Landing. This meant two things: one, after seven years of living here she still thought she was a tourist, and two, I was in for a very long and boring afternoon of shopping.

I ordered the Ragin' Cajun Steampot. Bree ordered the Cheesy Chicken. We also split an order of spinach and artichoke dip for an appetizer. Yeah, she ordered chicken at a seafood restaurant, that rebellious streak rearing its ugly head again. Why do we have to go to a seafood restaurant for her to order chicken? Another question in a long list of questions that I have learned not to ask over the last twenty years. A few other questions on this list: Why is it impossible for her to enjoy any movie that contains horses, or swords? Why is time travel so hard for her to understand? Why can't she remember to push the button marked TV before pushing the button marked power to turn on the TV? Why does she not have time to put gas in her car on the way home from work, but has time to get gas on the way to work even if she is late for work? Like accepting that the FDA allows so much bone meal and rat turds in hot dogs, I've learned to accept Bree's peccadilloes and, if I'm being completely honest, to even enjoy them at times, but I would never tell her that.

*****

We had finished lunch and were about a half hour into the shopping portion of the afternoon. Bree was happy. Not the usual happy, but the type of happy that comes shortly after two Bahama Mamas with lunch. Her tolerance for alcohol was a lot less now than when we first met. Mine probably was too. I wouldn't really know. I hadn't had a drink in seven years. But I did know how low my tolerance was for shopping.

I've found over the years that the key to happiness while shopping together is to not actually shop together. For example, when Bree went into the bikini shop, I went into a store that sold nothing but hot sauce. When she went into the shoe store, I went into the practical joke shop. When she went into the clothing store, I went into the magic shop, and when Bree went into the lingerie store, I went into the lingerie store.

After going into almost every store on one side of Barefoot Landing it was time to head to the other side. We walked along one of the floating bridges that connect the shops on the north side to the shops on the south side of the pond.

The bridge swayed slightly over the shimmering water as we walked along. Bree carried two bags, one from Sand and Sun, and one from Burlington Shoes. Any other bags were tucked inside those two.

There wasn't a cloud in the sky and the air was still. I could feel the beads of sweat run down my back. The sun was bright and I was squinting. I looked over at Bree, who smiled. She had on a pair of gold-rimmed aviators. She looked great in aviators.

"I gotta grab some sunglasses at one of these shops before my headache comes back," I commented.

Bree scanned the row of stores just ahead. "I think there's a place right over the bridge. I need a new pair too."

"You already have a pair."

"I *need* another pair." She stuck out her tongue.

"I bet you do."

Bree reached over and grabbed my hand. I looked at her. She was staring straight ahead. I could see through the side of her sunglasses that she was squinting now, but not because of the sun.

"What's that guy doing?" she asked.

"What guy?"

She pointed ahead of us. "That guy, at the end of the bridge."

I looked to where Bree had pointed. We kept walking, but slower now. The man just stood there, his arms dangling simian-like at his sides. He was too far away to get a good look at his face.

"Is he staring at us?" Bree slowed, and pulled slightly at my arm.

26

"I don't know." I looked behind us. There was no one else on the bridge. I looked back toward the man. He hadn't moved. He was wearing dark slacks, denim maybe, and a long sleeved gray shirt. Not what someone should be wearing at this time of the year. His hair was dark and matted from sweat. We got a little closer. He was wearing large sunglasses. I still couldn't get a good look at his face.

I crossed over in front of Bree to put her at my left side and pushed my right wrist against my revolver just to remind myself it was hidden there at my waistline under my shirt. We were a little more than half way across the bridge. His face was pale. He had no expression.

"Jake, I'm scared."

"It's okay. Probably just—" I paused.

He slowly raised his arm. We stopped. I stepped in front of Bree. The man pointed his finger at us with his thumb pointing upward like a child pretending to point a gun.

"BANG!" he yelled. I felt Bree flinch behind me. Several people near the man looked toward him. He paid them no attention. The man lowered his arm, turned, and quickly walked away. I started to follow.

"Jake! Wait!" Bree cried out.

I looked back at her, then back toward the man. He was disappearing behind one of the many shops. I knew he was headed for the parking lot. "Walk to the end of the bridge and wait there for me." I took off running. I could feel the wooden bridge groan underneath me.

When I reached the point where I had lost sight of the man I slowed to a walk and peaked around the corner of the building toward the parking lot. He was gone. I stepped from the sidewalk to the blacktop and walked out into the parking lot. I slowly turned around looking in every direction. Nothing. I shaded my eyes with my hand. There was no one in the crowd that looked like him. There were no cars leaving the parking lot that raised my suspicion.

Then I spotted him three rows of cars over, climbing into the side door of a white Chevy van. I took off running as fast as I could. I reached the door just as he was sliding it closed. I quickly shoved my arm into the closing door. I winced in pain. I grabbed the edge of the door with my other hand and yanked it open.

There he was, crouched in the back of the van with the look of shock on his face. The same look quickly spread to my face as I realized it was the wrong guy.

"Oh, sorry," I said, "I thought you were someone else."

"Asshole!" I barely had time to move my fingers, still clinging foolishly to the door as he slid it closed.

I headed back in the direction of my wife, rubbing my forearm. When I got back she was sitting on a bench at the end of the bridge next to a carousel.

"Did you catch him?"

"No."

"What's the matter with your arm?"

"Nothing. Come on." I motioned in the direction of the car.

I popped the trunk and rolled my eyes at the amount of junk in Bree's trunk; a three foot long black, iron candlestick holder. Why? I don't know. A large plastic bag of clothes that she was taking to goodwill … two years ago, and a small bag of dog food. We don't have a dog.

She quickly moved things around to make room for the shopping bags. I waited for her to finish and then placed the bags inside.

"Should we tell someone?" Bree asked.

"Tell who? What would we tell them? 'Hey, some guy pointed his finger at us and yelled bang'?"

"Don't make fun of me. It scared me."

"I know. Don't worry about it. It was probably just some nut," I told her reassuringly.

We sat at the light, waiting. I reached over and put my hand on Bree's thigh.

"Can we just take a little drive?" she said, placing her hand atop mine. "I don't feel like going home yet."

"Sure."

We headed toward Myrtle Beach.

Chapter Five

We had spent the better part of an hour and a half driving in to Myrtle Beach and from one end of Ocean Boulevard to the other. We drove past all the shops and restaurants that we hadn't been to in years. Many of the shops were the same ones that were here from our very first visit; others came and went with the seasons.

We stopped once, paid for parking, and walked down to the beach. It was at that point that Bree decided we should head home and maybe spend a few hours on the beach. It was at that point that I regretted paying ten dollars to park for only ten minutes.

I talked her into walking over to a cozy ice cream shop and grabbing a cone before we left. That way, I felt as though the ten dollars for parking was justified in some small way. I got cookies and cream, Bree got peanut butter swirl. We sat on a bench in a small park and indulged ourselves in the time-honored, and often nasty, sport of people watching.

"Gawd, look at the eighties hairdo on that lady," observed Bree wickedly. "You could hide a poodle under that hair-helmet!"

I chuckled. "Look over there, socks with sandals. Wish those socks were a little longer. Those varicose veins look like a Rand McNally map."

She laughed and said, "Coming this way, guy in jean shorts with his T-shirt tucked in."

We both laughed. We finished our cones and left.

*****

After arriving home Bree grabbed a beach blanket and a couple of towels. I went to the garage and got a small cooler to fill with ice and beer … and soda. I also filled a large beach bag with a radio, a book, a bag of pretzels, and two beer koozies. We changed into our bathing suits and walked to the beach.

I lay on my back, propped up on my elbows, looking out at the ocean. My feet hung past the towel, and I dug my heels into the warm sand. I was watching two kids ride the waves in on their boogie boards. *That used to be fun*, I remembered. I wondered if I would look foolish at my age being on a boogie board out in the water by myself. Answer: Of course I would.

Three seagulls were fighting over a piece of a sandwich someone had dropped—, ham, I think. It was a short fight. One quickly flew away with the bread. The other two bounced around, looking for something that may have been left behind. They squawked loudly at the loss of the sandwich. The two rats with wings walked toward me. One was eyeing my bag of pretzels. *Don't even think about it.*

The lifeguard blew his whistle. I looked up at him. He was giving that universal lifeguard *you're out too far* gesture with his arms. I looked to the water. Two young boys were swimming back toward shore. They were shaking their heads in disgust. They probably couldn't understand why the lifeguard wouldn't let them drown. I remembered wondering the same thing when I was a kid. The boys were probably having the same discussion every kid has in this situation. *It's the ocean, man. He don't own it. How can he tell us where we can swim and where we can't?* Yeah, kids are stupid, and at that age I was stupid, too.

A young girl, probably nineteen or twenty, walked by, pushing a yellow cart with a large blue umbrella attached to the side. She had light brown hair and light brown skin to match. She wasn't thin, but she wasn't fat. However, the blue bikini she wore was either bought one size too small or she had put on a few pounds since college began. She had full cheeks, lips, and ass, but her breasts were small. She was barefoot. I took in all these details and came to my usual conclusion: All girls in their late teens were pretty, even the borderline homely ones. This one had a cute heart-shaped face and the pleasingly plump factor didn't hurt her either.

"Italian ice!" she barked, a little self-consciously I thought. I looked to Bree.

"You want one?" I asked.

"One what?"

"A teenage girl," I responded sarcastically. "An Italian ice."

"No, thanks."

"'K." I watched as the young girl made her way down the beach. Other men my age watched too, but they weren't buying either. They were only browsing ... and wishing. They were remembering back to a time when they might have had a chance.

One guy nudged his buddy in the ribs and nodded his head toward the young girl. They both stared. One said something and the other laughed and shook his head yes. I didn't need to hear them to know what they were probably saying. *Note to self: If I ever have a daughter she will not be allowed to walk up and down the beach in a bikini selling anything.*

A few moms walked up to the cart with their kids leading the way. She handed each child a cup full of colored ice, took their money, and moved on.

"I'm sweating," I said.

Bree said, "Maybe you shouldn't have stared so long."

"Maybe," I replied. "You want to go in the water?"

"No. I just want to lay here and relax."

"'K." I got up and walked toward the water.

I walked out to where the water was chest-deep. No need in pushing it. I didn't want the whistle blown at me. That's embarrassing when you're in your forties. I pulled my feet up from the bottom and let myself sink below the surface. The water was cool and felt good after sweating on the beach. *I wonder if I can stay under long enough to worry the lifeguard. Probably not. He's a professional.* I stayed under as long as I could, then popped up quickly. I was facing away from the beach. I wiped the water away from my face and ran my hands across the top of my head. I looked toward the lifeguard. Just as I thought, he wasn't concerned.

I dunked my head under the water one more time, came up, and looked in Bree's direction. She lay in the same position. I floated in the water on my back, my toes just above the surface and my arms at my side treading water, while I watched her lying there on the sand. A vision, she was. I imagined she was a beached mermaid whose fishlike enchantment had worn off on dry land. I wondered what it would be like to make love to a mermaid. Guess only Tom Hanks would know.

Children ran around in delirious pleasure, playing tag and Frisbee and just generally enjoying the magic of being kids on the beach. Adults walked along holding hands, idly picking up shells, and relishing the sensation of hot sand squishing between their toes.

A man was kneeling in the sand between Bree and me. He had a stick and was writing in the sand. A jogger ran by. I watched the jogger. *If I could run like that, Bree could never keep up with me.* I looked back toward my wife. The man who was writing in the sand, stick still in hand, was now kneeling behind Bree. I felt a chill run through my body. Shit, he was looking through our beach bag! The sun was too bright. I was squinting. I couldn't make out a face. *Where did I leave those sunglasses?* He rose and stared right at me. He lifted the stick above his head in both hands and pretended to hit Bree over and over again. She lay there unaware, eyes closed. I looked to the lifeguard. He stood at the side of his chair, chatting up a girl whose boobs could double as the rescue tubes hanging from the lifeguard's chair.

I started making my way toward the shore as quickly as I could, feeling the mighty ocean turning my legs to lead. It was like running in a dream. I couldn't make myself move quickly enough. I thought about yelling, but didn't. The man looked up and saw me moving toward him and turned and quickly ran up the access path.

By the time I got to Bree the man was long gone. I stood over her and watched her chest move as she breathed. She opened her eyes.

"What the heck are you doing?" She asked.

"Nothing. Just watching you."

"Uh, OK. Is everything alright?"

"Everything is fine." *Big fat liar.*

She closed her eyes. I looked up the pathway.

I walked over to the beach bag and picked it up. Nothing was missing. My money clip was still there, as was both of our cell phones. I put the bag down and walked over to where he had been writing in the sand. In all capital letters it read.

"WHOS NEXT?"

Chapter Six

Who's next, I wondered as I sat in my recliner watching *Hawaii Five-0* on Me-TV, that station for old farts. As usual, I was amazed at how Jack Lord as Steve McGarrett managed to maintain that awesome hair flip from episode to episode. It was almost eleven o'clock. Bree lay on the couch, her head on the armrest, her legs curled up under a small blanket.

I didn't tell her about the man on the beach. The weirdo at Barefoot Landing was enough excitement for one day. I couldn't help wondering if the two were connected. In both cases the men were too far away to get a good look at their faces. On the beach the sun was in my eyes. I couldn't tell if the clothing was the same. Could they have been the same man? It was possible, but I wasn't going to start jumping to any conclusions. There's a lot of wackos out there. Maybe we just ran into two of them on the same day.

"You ready for bed?" I asked Bree. I could see her eyes were staying closed a little longer with each blink.

"Yeah. Let me wash my face."

She got up and went to her bathroom to start her nightly face-washing ritual. It involves about five products used in a certain order. I've stood there numerous times watching in fascinated appreciation as she expertly applies the "age defying" formulas. I pick on her a little about it, but at the same time I figure it's why she looks years younger than most women her age. I don't really know what's in those magical tubes and bottles, but they seem to work.

I'm usually in bed about ten minutes before Bree. My ritual of taking a leak is nowhere near as long as her face-washing ritual. I had turned on the nineteen inch television that hangs on the wall in our bedroom and also turned on the fan. The fan isn't for cooling, it's for sound. Bree can't sleep without it. She says if it's too quiet she can't sleep. It never made much sense to me in the beginning, but now I can't sleep without it either.

"Should I set the alarm?" she said as she walked into the room.

"Did you want to run in the morning?"

"Yeah, but we'll just go when we wake up."

"That's fine with me."

She kept her pajama bottoms on and slid into bed next to me. She put her head on my shoulder and her hand on my chest. Getting into bed with her pajama bottoms on was wife-speak for *you aren't getting any of this two nights in a row, buster.*

Chapter Seven

Even without the alarm I woke up at six-fifteen. I lay there for a while wondering if I should try this morning for what had eluded me the night before. I looked over at Bree. She was sleeping soundly, her mouth slightly open, with a little bit of drool in the corner. Her hair looked like it had been run through a Cuisinart. She made such a peaceful and slightly scary picture that I decided to get up and get dressed. *Maybe tonight.*

I went to the bathroom and splashed water on my face and through my hair. I looked in the mirror and thought about shaving. *Maybe tomorrow.*

I started to walk down and get the paper but then decided to drive. After getting the paper I drove to Krispy Kream for a dozen doughnuts. By the time Bree emerged from the bedroom I had drunk two cups of coffee, eaten five doughnuts, and was more than halfway through the crossword puzzle.

"Did you want to run?" she asked, yawning luxuriously and scratching her behind.

"Ugh. I ate too many doughnuts," I confessed, holding my sticky hands, stained with glazed goodness, up guiltily.

"Did you leave any for me?"

"There's five or six left in there," I said, pointing at the box. "Help yourself."

She opened the box. "No chocolate?"

"Just glazed."

"Chocolate is my favorite."

"I know."

"But you didn't get any?"

"I forgot."

"Out of sight, out of mind," she responded, jokingly.

"Only if I'm in a doughnut shop … or the Playboy Mansion," I shot back.

She ate the glazed sinker as though it was her new doughnut of choice, as well as the next two. "Go for a walk?" she asked, licking her fingers.

"Sure, let me jump in the shower first."

After taking my shower I wrapped a towel around my waist and walked out into the hall. Bree was sitting at the table reading the paper. "Hey, sexy" I said in what I hoped was my best erotic tone.

She looked up. "What?"

I opened the towel.

"Cool," she replied, and went on reading.

I knew she was impressed. She was probably just at a loss for words.

*****

We walked up Twenty-Fifth toward North Kings Highway. *A lot cooler this morning. We should have run today,* I thought.

Bree said, "We should have run this morning. It's a lot cooler out."

"Yeah," I said.

"Oh yeah, remember that woman in the paper that they found dead in her house over on First Avenue yesterday?"

"I remember." I knew where this was going. I had already read the paper.

"We did know her. She worked at the Circle K down the street. They said she was murdered."

"Huh."

"Someone kicked in her front door. They found her tied to a chair. She was shot and her throat was cut."

"Huh."

"'Huh'? Someone we know has their throat cut and all you have to say is 'huh'."

"What do you want me to say? It was horrible, I know … I need some cigars," I said, trying anything to change the subject. We took a left onto North Kings Highway.

I bought three cigars at Nicks: a La Unica 300 Natural, a Punch Double Corona, and a La Finca. I also grabbed a pack of Backwoods. The first three were for treating myself, the Backwoods were for any other occasion.

Bree was quiet. I knew she was thinking about Helen Gere. I broke the silence. "Beach today?"

"Sure. After it warms up a little."

We walked up the driveway. "I think I'll run to the grocery store and pick up something to cook on the grill for dinner," I said.

"Sounds good. When you get back we'll go down to the beach for a while."

Chapter Eight

At Bi-Lo I had purchased a gallon of milk, a 12-pack of Sprite, a box of blueberry frosted Mini-Wheats, and Pop-Tarts, the kind with no frosting, the good kind. I also grabbed a loaf of bread, white bread, the kind I like, not that shitty wheat bread that Bree buys, and two sirloin steaks, Certified Angus. They were on sale for $5.99 a pound. I had no idea if that was cheap or not, but a sale's a sale.

After loading the groceries into the passenger seat of my black 2010 Ford F-150, I walked over to the liquor store to get Bree a bottle of Lambrusco. They only had the small bottle. I like buying the big bottle. The less times I'm in a liquor store, the better.

I drove down Kings Highway and took a right onto Twenty-Eighth. As I was about to make a left hand turn onto my street I noticed a patrol car and a white van parked in front of the Bay Watch Resort. The lights of the patrol car were flashing. There were several on-lookers. I decided not to turn down my street and went to see what was going on.

As I approached I could see the lettering on the van: NORTH MYRTLE BEACH ANIMAL CONTROL. A young man and woman in their bathing suits and carrying beach towels were standing off to the side of the patrol car. A uniformed officer with a note pad was asking them questions and writing in the pad. The woman looked as though she had been crying.

Another uniform that I recognized as Pat Murray was speaking with the animal control officer. I pulled my truck to the side of the street, got out, and walked toward them. The officer taking notes glanced toward me and then back to his note pad.

According to the patch on the animal control officer's shirt his name was Joe. He closed the rear door of the van as I approached.

"Hey, Jake," Pat said.

"What's going on, Pat?"

Pointing in the direction of the young couple he said, "Couple over there called in a nine one one. They were coming off the beach and heading back up to their room. The girl was gonna grab a paper out of the machine over there. When she opened the door there was a dead dog stuffed inside. Blood all over the newspapers. A real mess."

"Jesus Christ." I could feel the hairs on the back of my neck stand up. "I got my paper out of that same box this morning." My shoulders tensed and I shivered a little.

"What time was that?"

I looked at my watch. "Maybe … three hours ago."

"Sick bastards," Joe declared, shaking his head as he approached Pat and me.

The younger officer finished up with the couple and joined us. "I took down all of their information, Pat. Should I let them go back up to their room?"

"Yeah, go ahead Gary," Pat said.

Gary turned and yelled to the couple, "You guys can go back up to your room."

"Don't yell at em, Gary," Pat said through clenched teeth and shaking his head. "Walk over and tell them. Christ."

Gary turned and started to walk back over to the couple.

Pat sighed heavily. "Not now, Gary. Next time."

"Oh, uh, yeah, I see what you mean. Sorry, Pat."

"It's fine, Gary. Now go in the trunk and get some rubber gloves and a plastic bag so we can take those bloody newspapers out of the machine."

"New?" I asked, nodding my head toward Gary when the kid was out of ear shot.

"Last week," Pat replied. "Officer Gary Finder, fresh from the academy. Rock bottom of his class. Good kid, conscientious and eager to please, but he's dumber than a board."

I laughed. Gary returned with the items Pat had sent him for. He held them out to Pat.

"*I'm* not gonna do it," Pat said.

I laughed again. I couldn't help it.

"Sorry, Pat. Uh, I'll do it right."

I could sense Pat was counting to ten before he said, "Stop saying you're sorry. Christ."

Gary walked up to the machine, bent over, and looked inside. "What kind of dog is it?" he gulped, struggling, I could tell, with keeping his breakfast down.

"A dead one," Joe said, as he climbed into his van.

Chapter Nine

It was one o'clock by the time I got home, put the groceries away, and Bree and I made our way down to the beach. We had brought the usual: beach towels, beach blanket, radio, a cooler with a couple beers for Bree, and a couple of sodas for me.

Bree reached over and grabbed a beer out of the cooler. I could smell the pungent goodness of the beer the instant she popped the top. I looked away.

"Do you still miss it?" she asked.

"The alcohol?" I asked as if I didn't know what she was asking about. "Every day. When I smell it I miss it. When I see it I miss it, when I walk in the door from work I miss it. Every time I have a cigar and have to drink a god-damn ginger-ale I miss it." I realized my voice was growing louder as I rambled. I stopped abruptly, then added "Yeah, I miss it," in a softer tone.

"Would you rather I didn't drink in front of you?"

"I think it's better that you *do* drink in front of me. I think the more I'm challenged, the stronger I become. If you only drank when I wasn't around I would feel like you were doing something behind my back."

She took a big gulp. I could almost taste it. Everyone has heard the line, "You don't have to drink to have fun." I used to think that was a lie. Now after *not* drinking for the past few years, I'm *certain* of it. Sure, I've had fun since I quit drinking. But I can remember things being a lot *more* fun when I did drink.

A shrink once told me that it was all in my head that I just thought I was having more fun because I was drunk. When he told me that, I remembered thinking, isn't that what fun is, all in your head? If you think you're having fun, aren't you probably having fun? But, he was a doctor and I was a drunk, and even though Willie Nelson sang, "There's more old drunks than there are old doctors," I chose to listen to the doctor. Sorry, Willie.

I reached for a ginger-ale. *Seven friggin' years.* I popped the top and took a sip. *Yum.*

I looked over at Bree lying there with her eyes closed, her eyelids slightly fluttering. She was wearing a black bikini today, with gold trim. Small beads of sweat sat on her cheeks and her chest just above her top. I looked down her stomach, stopped for a second at her belly ring. Her hipbones lifted her bikini bottom away from her body about half an inch. I tilted my head to see if I could see anything.

"What are you looking at?" she asked. I noted the subtle Mona Lisa grin on her face.

"Nothing," I said. I looked up at her. Her eyes were already closed again, but she was still smiling. I smiled, too, and looked out over the water.

"How long did you want to stay down here?" I asked.

"Why, are you getting bored?"

"No, just wondering."

The Italian ice girl was making her way down the beach again. I reached back into the beach bag and grabbed my money clip.

"I'm gonna get an Italian ice. You want one?" I asked.

"No," Bree replied. "Just tell her I said hello."

"Yeah." I stood up. I thought about putting my shirt back on but settled on sucking in my stomach.

I arrived at the cart at same time as a young boy I had seen earlier playing on the beach near us. He had light hair, cut very short. He was wearing blue Hawaiian print swim trunks. The white draw string hung out the front almost to his knees. He was very tan. Dry white sand clung to his shoulders. I stepped back to let him order first. He saw me step back and he did the same.

"Not getting one?" I asked.

"No. Just looking," he replied.

"You want one?"

He shrugged his shoulders. "I don't care."

"I don't care either. You want one or not?"

He blushed. The young girl waited impatiently, shifting her weight from one foot to the other. "Look, kid, I gotta keep movin'," she complained. "The boss don't like it if I stay in one place all day."

The boy looked at the girl and then at his feet. "Yes," he finally replied.

I looked around. "Where's your mother?" The boy pointed. The mother was already getting up from her beach towel. She was a very large woman with short brown curly hair. Her thighs were too big even for a woman her size, and her arms seemed a little too short. She sported amazing bingo wings, enormous sacks of flab that hung like fleshy hammocks between her elbows and shoulders. She wore a black one-piece bathing suit with a white ruffle around the waist. She waddled toward us like a distressed T-rex searching for her young.

"Can I buy him an Italian ice?" I called out.

Ms. Bingo wings looked puzzled. "Why?" she yelled back.

"Because he would like to have one, and I would like to buy him one." I replied.

She was almost to us. Christ, she really did look like a T-rex! Maybe if I stood real still she wouldn't see me, like the one in *Jurassic Park.*

No such luck. She looked at the young saleswoman, and back at me.

"I can buy my own son an ice cream," she announced haughtily.

"It's an *Italian ice*," the boy corrected her.

"Shut up! I know what it is, Ricky," she said. She grabbed Ricky by the arm. He flinched as her tiny doll-like hand reached for him. She escorted him back to his beach towel next to hers. He was getting the *never talk to strangers* lecture. I glanced over at Bree, she was watching. When she saw me look she closed her eyes and lay back down.

I looked back toward Ricky and his mother. The small boy stared at me as his mother's lips flapped out his scolding. He didn't look happy, but he probably didn't know the bullet he had dodged. Sometimes a T-rex will just eat their young.

I turned back to the girl and shrugged. "Just one, I guess." She gave me a little smile.

I returned to the beach blanket and plopped down.

"Causing trouble?" Bree asked.

"Just tried to buy that kid an Italian ice."

"The nerve."

His … uh. His … name was … Ricky," I said.

Chapter Ten

I, just like every other man in the world, love that sound when cold raw beef hits the red-hot grill. I can only imagine the first time some caveman decided to cook the meat instead of eat it raw. The first time he slapped that slab of meat down on to a hot rock and heard the sound of the flesh sizzling and that instant, glorious smell. I just know he turned to his hairy, squatting, grunting buddy next to him and high fived him. Then they both sat there watching the meat cook and wishing that someone would hurry up and invent beer.

I sprinkled some onion powder, some salt, pepper, and a little garlic powder on each steak. *Smells as good as it sounds.* I was sure every person within three hundred yards could smell those steaks and was just as envious as I was when I smelled someone else's grill. I closed the lid and picked my drink up off the table behind me. My drink this afternoon was Sprite in a rocks glass with a lime wedge. Some days, when I wanted a drink real bad, I drank my soda this way. It seemed to fool me into thinking it was a real drink. By real, of course, I mean booze.

I kicked off my flip flops and sat at the edge of the pool with my feet in the water. It was getting cloudy and the temperature had dropped about ten degrees. The weather man had said the high was supposed to be around fifty-eight for the next two days with a chance of rain both days. Rain makes for a shitty vacation, but I had six days left.

Bree called out the kitchen window, "I'm coming out in a sec, you want anything?"

"Yeah could you bring me my book and my glasses?"

"Sure, babe." She disappeared from the window. I looked up at the clouds. They were getting thicker.

"It's getting colder," Bree said, hugging herself as she handed me my book and glasses. "You want a sweater?"

"No, thanks" I replied.

Bree looked at my rocks glass sitting beside me. "You okay?

"I'm fine."

"Thinking about that boy?" Boy, she was shrewd.

"Yeah."

Bree put her hand on my head. She squatted down. Her hand went to the back of my head and then found its way to the back of my neck. She squeezed. She leaned in and kissed me above my ear. "I love you," she said.

"When she called him Ricky it felt like someone stabbed me in the heart."

"I know."

"He would be ten this summer."

"I know."

"What the hell?" I whispered, and rubbed my eyes with my thumb and finger. "I've got something in my eye."

I turned away so Bree couldn't see my tears. I still held onto the archaic notion that men shouldn't cry. Especially big bad cops.

When Bree drew me close, though, I didn't bother to keep it in.

Chapter Eleven

I awoke Friday morning with my feet sticking out from under the covers. They felt like ice cubes. *I must have forgotten to turn off the air conditioner.* My head was under my pillow. I could hear the rain hitting the window. *It must be windy.* I kept my eyes closed and pulled my feet up under the blankets. *I wonder what time it is?* I slid my feet over to warm them against Bree's legs__, always a bad move, sure to get me hit but she is always warm. I moved my feet around her side of the bed searching for warmth. It wasn't there. I pulled the pillow off my head and looked around the room. Bree was nowhere to be seen. I put my head back down and pulled the pillow back in place over my head.

The second time I awoke that morning was to a loud crash or bang or something. Who knows? I woke up after the noise, not before. I called to Bree. No answer.

I pulled on my pajama bottoms and a T-shirt and made my way to the kitchen. The broom lay on the floor. Mystery solved. I stood it back up against the wall. The kitchen door was open.

"Bree?" I called out again. No answer. I grabbed my sweater off the back of the chair and put it on as I walked toward the open door. "Bree?"

"What?"

"Jesus Christ! Don't sneak up behind me like that." She had come from the living room.

"Sorry."

"The doors standing open," I said, for lack of anything else to say.

"No kidding. I was just out there. They left us a paper by accident," she answered, handing me the *Sun News*.

"They who?"

"Well, duh, whoever delivers the paper, I guess."

I took the paper. "Good, I won't have to go out in the rain and get one." I threw it on the table and went to the coffee maker. Bree went to the door and closed it.

I said, "You want me to make something for breakfast."

"Sure."

I grabbed a pen off the counter and tossed it next to the paper and opened the fridge.

"You want eggs over medium or an omelet?" I asked.

"Omelets would be good." She sat down and started going through the paper.

I grabbed the eggs, butter, and milk out of the fridge and placed them on the counter next to the stove. I bent over and opened the cupboard and took out a large and a small frying pan and placed them on the stove. I opened the freezer and took out some frozen sausage links, unwrapped them, placed them on a small plate and put them in the microwave. I punched in one minute, and then plopped some butter into the large pan. I cracked open four eggs into a bowl and beat them beyond recognition, added a little milk, beat them some more and set them aside. The microwave dinged.

I took the sausage and dumped them into the small pan and set the flame on low. I opened a small can of mushrooms and dumped them into the melted butter, grabbed the handle and flipped them around, then added parsley, garlic powder, and onion powder. Flipped them again and turned the fire to low. A savory aroma filled the homey kitchen and set my taste buds afire.

"Music?" I asked.

"Sure," she answered.

I went to the living room and turned on the CD player. Jimmy Buffett started singing "Nobody from Nowhere."

"Ugh," I hear Bree say from the kitchen.

"It's good cooking music," I said defensively, and returned to my post at the stove.

I flipped the mushrooms one more time and added the egg and turned the fire down a little more. Then I flipped the sausage as I sang along with Jimmy.

"We must have gotten a used paper," Bree said.

I looked over. "What do you mean?"

"Someone wrote in it," she said. I walked over. She pointed at the paper.

She was right. Someone had taken a black marker and circled an article at the bottom of the last page and wrote "#3" in the middle of the circle. I leaned in closer to read the headline:

GEORGIA COUPLE FINDS DEAD DOG IN NEWSPAPER STAND.

I didn't need to read the article. I already knew that story. "Weird," I said, and went back to the stove to check breakfast. I glanced back at Bree. She folded up the newspaper. *Thank God, she's decided not to read the dead dog story.*

I went back to the fridge and got out the shredded cheese and sprinkled some on the eggs, then folded them over. Then I turned off the flame under both pans. I got two plates out of the cupboard and placed half of the omelet on each plate and then did the same with the sausage.

*****

After we ate I scraped the dishes and put them in the sink. I decided to use, "taking the garbage out", as my excuse to look around the house. So I did. I walked to the end of the driveway and looked up and down the street. Then I moved to the corner and looked up Twenty-Fifth Avenue. Nothing looked unusual.

I walked up Twenty-Fifth to our driveway and then around the side of the house. I looked over the fence into the pool. As I walked back I noticed something under the bush next to the driveway. I walked over and bent down. It was a wet newspaper. I picked it up. It was Monday's paper. I knelt down and unfolded the paper. On the front page an article was circled with "#2" in the center. The article read,

NORTH MYRTLE BEACH WOMAN SHOT DEAD IN HER HOME.

Chapter Twelve

I tossed both newspapers on Merle's desk. Merle is Captain Merle Stein, a lifelong resident of North Myrtle Beach. Merle was tall, about six-three. He was average weight for his size. He had dark black hair, black as a crow's ass, and all one color, not a smidgen of gray. It was obvious Merle inherited his hair color from his Uncle Just-For-Men. He wore it slicked back tight to his head. He had dark skin with deep laugh lines around his eyes and three deep wrinkles across his forehead. His eyebrows were thick and long, shooting off in every direction like squashed caterpillars. He always wore a long-sleeved white shirt no matter what the occasion or what the temperature was outside, and he always wore a tie. I remember three times he and his wife, Margot, showed up at my house for a cookout and pool party. Captain Merle Stein wore a long-sleeved shirt and tie all three times.

His office door was open so I had just walked in. The wet papers hit the desk with a thud. Merle, sitting at his desk jumped, at the sound, spilling his coffee down the front of his clean white shirt.

"Goddammit!" he shouted. "Can't you knock?" Merle reached for the napkin under a powdered doughnut that lay on his desk.

"The door was open," I returned.

"What the hell are these?" He dabbed at the coffee stain as though the napkin was made from some kind of New Age, miracle paper. *Billy Mays here, folks! Let me introduce my new Miracle Napkin! Gets out coffee stains, red wine, and even pesky blood stains blood stains! Only $19.99!*

"They're newspapers, Merle," I said.

"I *know* they're newspapers. What are you, a paperboy on your days off?"

"No," I replied as I leaned over his desk to open the newspapers.

He said, "Look at my shirt."

I said, "*Look* at these newspapers."

"This stain will never come out."

"Will you look at these papers, please?"

He glanced at them, still wiping his shirt. "What am I looking at?"

"The circles around these articles."

"Yeah, so? You circled a couple stories in the paper."

I pointed at the story about Helen Gere. "Ya see this? This woman was murdered in her house a few days ago."

He leaned closer to the paper, stabbed it with a pudgy finger. "I know. Gere. Over on First Avenue. She was shot in the head. Whoever did it also cut her throat. The coroner said the throat was cut first, then she was shot. Said the cut would have killed her pretty quick. Don't know why they shot her too. She worked at a convenience store or something."

"Yeah, I know. I knew her, spoke to her a couple times a week."

"That's too bad, Jake, but why did you circle the story? Why are you tell—"

"I didn't circle it. Someone else did, and left it at my house. You see here … inside the circle, there's a number two. And here," —I slid the other paper over in front of him—. "this story here … a number three inside the circle."

Merle read the story and looked back at me. "You know the dog, too, Jake?" he asked.

"No, I didn't know the dog, Merle, but someone left that dog in the same newspaper stand where I get my paper almost every morning while I'm on vacation."

"And you think it was left there on purpose so you would find it? And you think it has something to do with the Gere murder? That's kind of a stretch, Jake."

"Listen, Merle, someone left those papers at my house. Someone circled those stories, and someone numbered them two and three. That makes *me* think there might be a four or five."

"What happened to number one?"

"I don't know."

Merle leaned back in his chair and folded his fingers behind his head. "Jake, come on. There's a lot of mights and maybes in that theory. Besides, what do you want me to do at this point? We're looking into the Gere thing. I'll have a uniform look into the dog. Go home, Jake. You're on vacation. Go take your wife somewhere nice for a couple days. Go home."

I can be as stubborn as a bulldog when I want to be. "Who's working on the Gere murder?"

"Chandler."

"By himself?"

"No, I put him with Lint while you're on vacation."

Sam Chandler was my partner. We had inherited each other two years ago when both of our previous partners coincidentally retired on the same day. Sam was a good cop. Smart, a quick thinker. Avis Lint, on the other hand, was a moron. I didn't like the idea of the two of them being partnered up. I was afraid Sam might catch a bad case of stupid from Lint.

Avis Lint had been with the North Myrtle Beach police department for thirty-five years, and he was dumber now than the day he walked out of the academy. He was fat and he was lazy. Lint had eight kids from three marriages. Almost every dime he made went to child support or alimony. He was a miserable bastard. Half the guys on the force wondered why he hadn't put a gun in his mouth yet, and the other half wished he would.

"Lint. Just great," I sighed.

"Just go home, Jake."

Chapter Thirteen

Merle had said to go home, and that was probably a good idea. Instead, however, I found myself sitting in my truck and my truck found itself sitting in a parking lot off of Bamwell Street.

Helen Gere lived in a small two-bedroom two-bathroom townhouse at the corner of First Avenue and Bamwell. Her townhouse was part of a development that ran from Elm Avenue to Bamwell Avenue and from Third Avenue to First Avenue South. There were about thirty-five or forty buildings with four or five units per building. Helen's building had five units; hers was all the way at the end toward First Avenue.

From my truck I could see which unit was Helen's. There were strips of yellow plastic tape that crisscrossed her front door. I couldn't read the black lettering from my truck, but I knew it didn't say CAUTION-WET PAINT.

I got out of my truck and walked up the winding concrete path that led to her door. I tried the doorknob. I knew it was probably locked but tried it any way. It was unlocked. I pushed it open, staying behind the yellow tape.

"She's not home," came a voice from behind me.

I hope not. I turned. A small blue-haired woman stood at the door across from Helen's. Her husband, at least a foot and a half taller than her, loomed behind her, peering suspiciously over her head. He looked remarkably like an aged turtle craning it's wrinkly neck for a grape that was just out of reach.

"She's dead," he called out.

"I know," I responded.

"Then why are ya here?" the old woman asked.

"I'm a cop."

The old lady folded her arms across her saggy bosom. "Sure ya are."

"Got any ID?" hubby demanded.

"Yes," I responded, walking toward them. The old man put his hand on the woman's shoulder and gently pulled her back out of the doorway. He moved around her and made his way in my direction. I reached into my back pocket and pulled out my wallet. He reached out with his long boney, crooked fingers and took the wallet from me. He squinted at the badge and ID, and handed it back to me.

"Sorry," he said. "We're all a little jumpy around here since Helen was killed. Cut her throat they said, and then shot her in the head."

"Who told you that?"

"The other cop. Heavy guy. Lintz, or something."

"Lint."

"Yeah, that's him. Lint."

The old man reached out his hand. "Orville Garmin," he said. I shook his hand.

"Jake Stellar."

"Jake Stellar," he said my name slowly and grinned. "Sounds like one of those made-up names. Like a cop on TV or something. Jake Stellar, private eye," he laughed. At the end of his laugh came a long wheeze and a cough.

I shook my head. "So I've been told."

He pointed back toward his house. "Well, if you need anything we'll be in the back yard over there. There's a gate on the side." He turned and headed back toward his front door. "Jake Stellar," he repeated with a chortle. "See ya on the boob tube."

I returned to Helen's front door. I stepped over one piece of yellow plastic tape and ducked under the other, so as not to disturb it. I was inside. I looked around. The place was quiet. Every house is quiet when no one is home, but when you know they're not home because they're dead it just seems that much quieter.

In the middle of the living room floor there was a large dark stain. It's hard to believe there's that much blood in the human body. They say it's about six quarts but it looks like six gallons when it's spilled out on to a beige shag carpet. I walked around the stain to the opposite wall where an oak mantle decorated the wall over a fake fire place. There were framed family pictures on the mantle and an American flag folded into a triangle in a display case. Next to the flag was a black and white photo of a young man in uniform, Vietnam era. Probably her husband, I guessed. There were two faded photos of babies and one of a woman in her early forties or late thirties with two children. There was a picture of a dog lying under a Christmas tree. I had seen that dog before, stuffed in a newspaper box. I wondered if Sam had made the connection yet. I knew Lint hadn't, but what was the connection to me?

I made my way through the dining room into the kitchen. I looked in cupboards. I looked in drawers. I looked in the stove, under the stove, under and in the fridge. I closed the fridge and looked at the door. There were magnets on the door. One from California Pizza, one from Hong Kong Chinese Restaurant, and one from an insurance company. A pen hung by a piece of yarn from a magnet. There was a Yankees schedule—, we had something in common. There was a game circled: Yankees at Twins, June third. She had a daughter up north somewhere. Minnesota, maybe?

Before leaving Helen's I snooped through both bedrooms and bathrooms. Didn't turn up anything there either.

I left her townhouse through the police tape the same way I had arrived. I made my way across First Avenue and into a small wooded area where I found a path through the trees. I followed the path, which exited into the rear parking lot of a strip mall that I immediately recognized as one anchored by a Kroger. There was no reason to walk around the front of the building. I knew what other stores were in the mall, and I knew Hong Kong Chinese Restaurant was one of them.

I turned back down the path, looking at the ground as I slowly walked along. I noticed some cigarette butts lying on the side of the path and crouched down. I counted the butts. Nine. I picked one up and read the filter: Marlboro. The writing was green. I stood back up and looked toward Helen's. I could see her front door and the entire side of her townhouse. Two windows upstairs, one window down.

I wondered if the killer had stood where I was standing now. I closed my eyes and imagined him standing here, watching her. I could feel the hair on my arms and the back of my neck stand up. I opened my eyes.

I walked back to my truck and got in. I leaned over and put the cigarette butt in the unused ashtray, started the truck, and left.

Chapter Fourteen

You have reached the voice mail of Sam Chandler. I'm not able to answer my phone right now. If you could leave your name, number, and a brief massage I'll get back to you as quick as I can.

"Sam, it's Jake. Hey, just wanted to touch base with you on the Helen Gere thing. Give me a call back when you get a chance." I hung up the phone.

"I thought you were on vacation?"

I turned and saw Bree standing behind me, arms crossed, hip pushed out.

"I am. I jus—"

"You just what? You just don't think that place can run without you? Bree asked.

"No. I just had a couple questions for Sam."

"About what?"

"About work."

"What about work?"

"Nothing. It's nothing important." I went to the cupboard for a rocks glass, then to the fridge for ice and a can of ginger-ale. *Man, I could use a drink.* I looked out the kitchen window. It was raining again. I went to the living room and turned on the TV and took my place in the recliner. I let the foot rest out and got comfortable. Bree followed me in.

"You want to talk about anything?" she asked.

"No."

"I heard you mention that woman's name on the phone."

"What woman?" I knew exactly what woman she was talking about.

Bree kicked the foot rest hard. "You know exactly what woman I'm talking about!"

"Oh, *that* woman. I just wanted to ask Sam if they had gotten any leads. I figured … you know … since we knew her I would just, you know, ask." *That didn't sound convincing.*

"You didn't seem too concerned yesterday. What's changed?"

"Nothing has changed. Can we just drop it, please?"

Bree turned and walked out of the room. "Fine," she said in a voice that meant it was anything but fine.

I took a big swig of my soda. *Yuck.* I took my cell phone out of my pocket and tried Sam's phone one more time. Got his voice mail again, didn't leave a message this time.

"Did you eat lunch?" I hollered in to Bree. No answer. *She's pissed.* "I didn't," I yelled, but a little quieter. Still no answer. *Christ.* I pulled myself up out of the recliner.

Bree was rinsing off the breakfast dishes I had scraped and was putting them in the dishwasher.

"I was wondering if you had eaten lunch," I said softly.

"I heard you. I was ignoring you."

"Why?"

"Because you're a dick," she answered. She had me there.

"Sorry." I walked over and put my arms around her. I grabbed her left breast with my right hand. "You love me?" I asked. I playfully bit her shoulder.

"I love you," she responded, turned and kissed my cheek.

"Should we go in the bedroom and you can show me how much?"

"That's why you apologized, because you're horny?"

"I wasn't horny till you put your boob in my hand." I pressed against her hip. "See, I'm ready."

"As much as that beautiful, glorious, irresistible thing pressed against my hip turns me on, I think I'll pass."

"Was there a little sarcasm in that?" I asked.

"Yeah, just a little." She broke free of my sex grip and returned to putting the dishes in the dishwasher.

Huh, I thought, *number one: house hold chores. Number two: sex with me. This woman has her priorities all messed up.* I walked back to the recliner to drown my sorrows in my ginger-ale.

"Yes, I ate lunch," she yelled in. "You?"

"No."

"Are you hungry?"

"A little."

"You want me to cook something or do you want to go out for dinner?"

"Whatever." I was pretending to pout about not getting sex.

"Are you pouting about not getting sex?" She called out.

"No." *I'm pretending to pout, so there.* She thinks she's so smart.

"We could get take-out."

"Yeah, I'll go pick up something and grab a movie to watch," I said.

"Sounds good. Then maybe later I'll sex you up," she giggled.

Done pouting.

Chapter Fifteen

With a little persuading on my part we had settled on Chinese food for dinner. With a little more persuasion, I had gotten her to order from The Hong Kong Chinese Restaurant. Why, I wondered did my powers of persuasion not work that well in the sex department?

On my way to pick up the food I went a little out of my way and drove by Sam's house. Sam lived alone in a house on Jordan Road, behind the school. The sun had gone down, but it wasn't quite dark yet. I drove by slowly, taking my foot off the gas and coasting. There were no lights on and his car wasn't in the driveway. I drove on to the restaurant.

"Order for Stellar," I said.

"One minute," the small Asian man behind the counter said.

"Yup."

He walked back behind a red curtain that hung in a doorway between the counter and the kitchen.

Ancient Chinese secret. Is that racist? I wondered.

Another man came to the counter. "I help you?" he asked with a wide grin.

"Order for Stellar."

"One minute," he responded, bowing slightly, and disappeared behind the same curtain.

Déjà vu, I thought. *Or maybe that's only at a French restaurant.*

After a short wait the second man reappeared from behind the curtain with a white plastic bag with the picture of a red dragon on it. "Order for Sterral," he said.

Too many Rs and Ls.

I took the bag and set it on the counter and pulled out my wallet. I flashed him my badge as I pulled out a fifty. "Maybe you can help me," I said. "Do you have a regular customer named Helen Gere?"

"You no Sterral?" he asked, cocking his head in puzzlement.

"Yes, I'm Stellar, but—"

"Order for Sterral," he said, pushing the bag toward me.

"Helen Gere," I said. "Do you have a regular customer named Helen Gere?"

"You Heren Geel?"

I scanned the room for help. A waitress was walking toward me.

"Excuse me, do you speak English?" I asked.

"We *all* speak English here," she replied with a smirk she probably reserved for smart-ass white people. "What can I help you with?"

The waitress was also Asian but with no accent what-so-ever. She was young, attractive, and very petite, with bright eyes and an intelligent face. Her long, straight black hair was pulled back into a ponytail. She was wearing black stretch pants and a white T-shirt that read "Hong Kong Chinese Restaurant" in flamboyant red letters.

"I just wanted to ask a few questions about a woman who may or may not be a customer of yours."

The waitress hesitated. "Well, we don't usually give out information about our customers."

I went to my back pocket once again for my badge. I flashed it. If she was impressed, she didn't show it. "Jake Stellar," I said, extending my hand.

She squinted and stretched her neck to get a better look at my ID. "Jake Stellar." She grinned. "Wasn't there a cop on TV named Jake Stellar?"

Get a grip, Jake. Don't say anything foolish. "No."

"Well, there should have been. It would have made a great cop name."

"It *is* a cop name," I said.

"Oh yeah, I guess it is. Who did you want to ask about?"

"A woman by the name of Helen Gere."

She went around to the computer screen above the cash register and typed in "Helen Gere."

"Here she is." She scrolled down the screen. "Orders about two or three times a month." Her eyes went back to mine. "Is she okay?"

"She was killed a few days ago. When was the last time she ordered?"

She scrolled back up the screen. "Monday. Four forty-eight p.m."

"How many delivery people work here?" I asked.

"We have two people who deliver. They're both part-time. And my uncle" —she pointed to the man behind the counter—, "he'll deliver if he needs to."

"Has anyone quit in the last few days?"

"Why are you asking about our employees?" She squinted and cocked her head. "Do you think someone here had something to do with this woman's murder?"

"I'm just asking. I'm not implying."

"No. No one has quit in the last few days."

"Does it say who delivered on Monday?"

She looked back at the screen. "No. Doesn't say. Sorry"

I noted she had no trouble with Rs. I picked up my bag of food. "Thanks for your help." I reached for my wallet once again, opened it, and removed my business card and handed it to her. She took it. "If you think of anything else please give me a call. My cell number is at the bottom."

"Anything else like what?" she asked, staring at the card and then back at me.

"Anything you didn't think of today," I replied. I turned and left.

I reached through the open window and placed the bag on the front seat of my truck and walked around the building to the path I had found earlier. It was dark now and quiet. The parking lot and the area behind the building were well lit. I made my way down the path. The path was dark. I wondered if Helen had ever used this path or even knew it existed. Did the delivery boy ever use the path? Did the killer follow Helen through the path one night? How many nights did the killer stand here planning and plotting the murder? How long did he stand here, smoking cigarettes? Did anyone see the glowing ash as the killer inhaled?

I stood at the end of the path. I looked at Helen Gere's house. I looked over at the Garmin's house. Their lights were on. Their shades open and curtains pulled back. The window was open. *Not too jumpy since Helen's murder*. Orville's wife walked by the window. *What was her name? Did he tell me?*

I returned to my truck and headed for home.

Chapter Sixteen

I awoke around seven on Saturday morning. Bree was still sound asleep so I got out of bed as quietly as possible. I made myself a cup of coffee, tried Sam's cell again. Got no answer. I walked down to the newspaper box and got the paper. There was no dog inside.

By the time Bree got out of bed I was half way through my second cup of coffee and had finished most of the crossword puzzle.

"Anything interesting?" Bree asked, nodding toward the paper as she walked by.

"Dagwood wants comment cards at the diner, Sarge beat the shit out of Beetle and twisted him into a pretzel, and we can ride all day for $24.99 at The Family Kingdom amusement park," I responded, never taking my eyes off of my crossword puzzle.

Bree walked to the kitchen window and pulled back the curtain. "It looks nice out."

"Maybe I'll leave it out," I responded, looking and pointing at my zipper.

"*What's wrong with you?*"

I put my finger to my lips and made a blubbering sound. "I have the mind of a child."

Bree said absently, "I wonder what the temperature is."

"I walked down to get the paper in just my T-shirt. It didn't feel too cold."

"*Just* your T-shirt?"

"What's wrong with *you*?" I asked.

"I'm married to a man with the mind of a child." Bree went to the living room and turned on the television and put it on the Weather Channel. "It's fifty-one. High today of seventy," she announced.

"Did you want to run?"

"Sure."

We put on our running clothes and running shoes and went out the front door. Standing in the driveway, Bree bent over and touched her toes. Of course, I looked at her ass. She looked at me upside down from between her legs and smiled. I walked over and leaned against a palm tree and stretched my legs. She went to the lamp-post and did the same.

"Ready?" she asked.

"As ready as I'll ever be."

"What way do you want to go?"

"I'll follow you."

She took a right out of the driveway and I followed. We ran all the way to the end of Hillside and took a right onto Twenty-Eighth. Then we took a right on Madison. As usual we ended our run on the beach and walked up through the Bay Watch Resort to South Ocean Boulevard and home.

"How far do you think we ran?" Bree asked.

"A little less than four miles."

As we walked up the driveway I scanned the yard for newspapers. *No newspapers, thank God.*

Bree went down the hallway as I headed toward the kitchen table to check my phone. "I'm gonna jump in the shower," she said. "Then we'll run and grab something to eat."

I said, "Sounds good," and picked up my cell. Five missed calls and one text message.

I read the text. It was from Merle. *Jake call me as soon as you get this*. I did. There was no answer. I left a message. "Captain, it's Stellar returning your message. Call me back."

I set the phone down. It rang instantly. "Hello?"

"Jake?"

"Yeah?"

"You home?"

"Yeah. What's up?"

"Stay there. I got a car on its way to pick you up."

"Why? What the he—" The phone went dead. "Captain?"

I tried to call Merle back but there was no answer. I put my phone in my pocket and went to the bathroom door.

"Bree?" I called through the door.

"Yeah?"

"Something has happened down at the station. Merle is sending a car for me. I don't know how long I'll be."

"What happened?" she yelled back over the sound of the running water.

"I don't know. I'll give you a call when I get there. Love you," I hollered back as I headed for the door.

"Love you, too."

As I walked down the driveway a patrol car pulled up. The driver was Gary… whatever. *Did Murray tell me Gary's last name. Who knows*? I got in the car.

Gary squealed the tires. My head snapped back. "In a hurry there, Gary?" I asked.

Gary didn't answer or make eye contact. For the first time I noticed that his hands were trembling on the steering wheel and his face was white as a ghost.

"Everything okay?" I asked.

"Yes… no. I mean… no, sir," he responded. His voice was shaky.

He turned right onto North Kings Highway and pushed his foot to the floor.

"You might want to turn on the lights," I said. He reached over and did so. He glanced at me and then back to the road.

We flew by Second Avenue without slowing at all. "I think you missed your turn, Gary."

"No, sir," Gary replied.

We slowed and took a right onto Eighth. Gary pushed his foot to the floor once again.

Shit! I thought. "Where are we going?" I asked. No answer from Gary. "Gary, where are we going?"

We took a left onto Jordan Road. There were cop cars everywhere. A fire department emergency truck and two ambulances. Gary stomped on the brake and slid to a stop in the gravel at the edge of the road.

I jumped from the car and ran up Sam Chandler's driveway. Captain Stein was walking out the front door.

"Merle!" I yelled.

Two officers yelled and tried to stop me. I broke through.

"Jake, stop!" Merle hollered.

I tried to run past him. He grabbed me by the arm and swung me around. His strength surprised me. Lint was there quicker than I thought he could move. He threw his arms around me from behind and squeezed. I couldn't move.

"Jake, wait," Lint demanded.

I elbowed Lint in the gut and broke free of Merle's grip. I ran through Sam's front door. "Where is he? Sam!" I called out.

A door that led from Sam's kitchen to the garage was open. The sun shined through the open garage door. I could see a silhouette in Sam's car. I knew right away it was Sam. I ran toward the car. A detective jumped in front of me and grabbed my shoulders. "Jake, it's too late. He's gone. Sam's gone."

The driver's side door was open. Sam sat in the front seat, his head tilted back. There was a blood trail from Sam's temple that ran down his neck to his shoulder. His throat was cut. Sam's blood and brain matter was splattered against the passenger side window.

I closed my eyes as hard as I could to make the image go away. I pushed the heels of my palms into my eye lids. I felt sick to my stomach. My head was spinning like I had drunk too much. I opened my eyes to stop the spinning. It didn't stop. My legs were weak I stumbled back against the garage wall.

Perkins still had me by the shoulders. He was supporting most of my weight. His grip was tight ... or I was weak. I couldn't tell. Dill Perkins's face was stressed, his eyes were red, and his jaw was tight. He slowly turned me and pushed me backwards into Sam's kitchen. I didn't resist.

"I was the first one on the scene," Dill said.

I opened my mouth but couldn't think of anything to say. I looked back over Dill's shoulder at Sam, his lifeless body frozen in his last micro second of life. *Open your eyes, Sam*, I thought. I felt a tear run down my cheek and quickly wiped it away.

"Keep it together, man," Dill said.

Really? Keep it together, man. That's your best line, Dill? What are we, in some shitty cop movie?

I broke free of Dill's death grip, turned and walked to the kitchen sink. I turned on the cold water and splashed it on my face, then grabbed a dishtowel hanging on the back of Sam's oven and wiped my face. I opened a cabinet looking for a glass. Wrong cabinet. There was a bottle of Crown Royal staring back at me. *Come on, Jake, one drink*, the bottle said. *One drink won't kill you. It will help you keep it together, Jake.* I passed and slammed the cabinet.

I turned back to Dill. "When did you find him? How long has he been there?"

"Lint tried to call him a couple of times last night, never got an answer. Sam was supposed to pick Lint up this morning at six. Sam never showed. Lint called the station to see if anyone had heard from Sam. No one had, so Gwen and I—" Dill didn't complete his statement. He motioned toward his partner, Gwen Lawrence who was sitting at Sam's dining room table. Gwen wasn't *keeping it together.*

Shit, Gwen. I stared at her from the kitchen. She sat in a chair leaning over, elbows on her knees. Her back was to us and her shoulders were shaking.

She and Sam had dated a few times. No one was supposed to know, but everyone did know.

"Gwen knew where Sam hid a key," Dill continued. "We knocked a few times. There was no answer so we came in. I found him in the garage. The coroner put time of death somewhere between five and eight last night."

"Any sign of—"

Dill shook his head briskly. "No sign of forced entry. No sign of a struggle. No sign of a robbery. Sam's gun is still holstered."

I took a deep breath, turned, and went back into the garage. I walked around the driver's side door, leaned over, and looked in at Sam. I felt a chill through my entire body. I hoped no one noticed. I pulled Sam's jacket open. There was his gun, still holstered just as Dill had said. I looked up on the dashboard, then in the back seat. Nothing. Not an empty coffee cup. Not an old McDonald's bag. No wadded up paper. I thought of our many arguments about Obsessive-Compulsive Disorder and smiled. I thought about all the times I had called him Detective Felix Unger. I was gonna miss Sam.

"Has anything been touched or moved?" I said to Merle, who had been inspecting the trunk. He reached in his coat pocket and pulled out a clear evidence bag. Inside was a pair of gold-rimmed aviator sunglasses.

Merle replied, "He was wearing these, but it appeared they had been put on him after he was shot. Gonna have the lab check for prints."

"You'll probably find my prints," I said.

"Why?"

"Because they're my sunglasses."

Merle looked puzzled. "Did you loan them to him?"

"No. They disappeared from my home a few days ago."

Dill approached. "How did they get here, Jake?" All eyes were on me.

"I have no idea."

Chapter Seventeen

It was well after midnight by the time a unit dropped me off back at my house. Bree had already been filled in on the situation. She knew Sam was dead. She didn't know exactly how. Of course, she didn't know exactly how Helen Gere was murdered either, and she didn't know anything about that god damn dog. She didn't know I suspected everything was connected to me, and she sure as hell didn't know this bastard had been in our home. I would keep that from her as long as possible. That was something she just didn't need to be thinking about.

Ricky's death ten years ago changed Bree. The death of a six-year-old son would change anybody. Hell, I spent three years trying to drink myself to death. His death affected her differently though. There was no drinking, no yelling, no noticeable breakdown. She didn't even cry that much. She cried a little the day of the accident, and a little bit the day of the funeral. Other than that she just didn't seem to grieve that much. She was just *different* after.

There was no other way to put it. Before the accident she was more outgoing. She was stronger, more sure of herself. Now she is more fragile, weaker somehow. If I would mention the change to friends or family members they would tell me I was imagining it. They all said she seemed the same to them, in fact, she seemed fine. I figured it was because they just didn't know her as well as I did. I told myself the change in her was so slight that only I noticed. They were right, she did seem *fine*, but not the *same*. A husband knows.

Before the accident, if we were about to leave the house, she would put on a sweater or jacket with no thought. Now, after the accident, she always asks, "Should I put on a jacket?" Or, "Do you think it's too cold for this shirt?" Before, if I asked her what she wanted for dinner, she knew what she wanted. Now, she wants my input. It's not like she wants it, it's like she needs it. She worries about oncoming storms, where before she didn't. All small changes I know, but changes none the less.

I find myself now trying to protect her from things. Not telling her sad news, not talking about my job unless it's something happy or humorous. I never bring home a sad movie especially one that might involve the death of a child. Sometimes I wonder if it's me who did all the changing. Maybe *me* taking on this protector roll changed *her*.

Bree was lying on the couch when I entered. Other than the light under the microwave and the glow of the television the place was dark. The volume of the TV was turned down low. I crept in so as to not wake her, just in case, but she was awake. She turned her head and looked up at me. She raised her hand. I took hold and squeezed. She tried to produce a slight grin. I did the same. Bree sat up, and I sat down next to her. She put her head on my shoulder.

"How are you holding up?" she asked.

"Good as can be expected, I guess."

"Do you want to talk about it?"

"No."

"Okay."

I tilted my head back, resting it on the back of the couch, and stared at the ceiling. I let out a long, loud sigh. Bree put her head on my lap and stretched back out on the couch. I reached up and pulled the small blanket off the back of the couch and spread it out over her.

"Angie go home?" I asked.

Angie was a friend of Bree's that lived around the corner. I called her first and asked her to go over to the house and sit with Bree so she wasn't alone when she got the news about Sam.

"Yeah. She looked tired so I told her to go home."

"How late did she stay?"

"About eleven, I guess."

"I noticed the empty bottle of Lambrusco on the table. I guess I should have gotten the large bottle."

Bree grinned. "Yeah, that didn't last very long. Luckily Angie brought a bottle too."

"Luckily," I echoed.

I leaned over and kissed Bree on the forehead. I slouched down a little in the couch and got comfortable. I leaned my head back and dozed off.

People always talk about their dreams. I never do, because I very rarely have them. That came up in therapy one time. My shrink said I dreamed just as much as everyone else. I just didn't remember them. He had some line about waking up at different stages of sleep or something, I don't know, I wasn't really listening. I was daydreaming probably. He also said something about alcohol inhibiting my memory of dreams. Of course, it always came back to alcohol. *Alcohol bad.*

This night, however, I did remember my dreams. I dreamed about Sam. I dreamed about being at his wake. I remember walking up to his casket. It was open. I remember wondering why they didn't cover up the hole in the side of his head or clean the blood off of his shirt. I wondered why they didn't dress him in a turtleneck to hide the gash in his throat.

I remember turning to Bree and asking her why they had put my sunglasses on him. She replied, "He loved wearing his Daddy's sunglasses."

I looked back at Sam but he was gone, and Ricky was lying in his place.

"He wants to be a cop when he grows up," Bree said. "He wants to be just like you. He wants to drink too much. He wants to kill people when he grows up. He wants to kill his own son. He wants to be just like you if he grows up."

Ricky opened his eyes and said, "I want to be just like you Dadd—"

I awoke with a start. My heart was pounding. I felt as though it was going to pound right out of my chest. I reached up and wiped the sweat from my forehead. My mouth was dry. I looked into the kitchen. I could see the empty bottle of wine sitting on the table. I turned back and stared at the ceiling until I fell back asleep.

Chapter Eighteen

Sometime during the night Bree and I had moved from the couch to the bedroom. I was up by five-thirty. I put on my black sweatpants that said "Captain Morgan" down the right leg in big red letters and my green Margaritaville Tequila t-shirt that said *tip it, flip it, sip it* in yellow and orange letters across the back.

I went into the bathroom and stood looking into the mirror. I thought about my dream. I thought about how much I already missed Sam. It's funny how you can go a few days without missing someone, but when you know you'll never see them again, you miss them every minute. I stared at the bags under my eyes from lack of sleep.

I turned on the cold water and splashed it on my face a few times, holding my cold fingers against the bags for a few seconds with each splash. I rubbed the last splash of water through my hair to tame the bed head. It didn't work. I didn't care.

I put on my brown leather house shoes and walked to the newspaper box. Another warm morning.

On my way back to the house I looked at the front page. There was a picture of Sam, in uniform. Underneath his picture it just said SAM CHANDLER. The headline at the top of the page read, NORTH MYRTLE BEACH POLICE OFFICER KILLED. The lead paragraph of the story said, "North Myrtle Beach police officer Samuel Chandler was found dead in his patrol car Saturday morning in the garage of his Jordan Road home, the victim of an apparent murder. According to Capt. Merle Stein, whose department is conducting a rigorous investigation, the veteran officer's throat had been slashed."

I read on. They had gotten the gory details of Sam's murder right, and they had gotten about 75 percent of his personal story right too. Never having had much respect for reporters, I figured the hack had filled in the parts he didn't know. They said Sam was a lifelong resident of North Myrtle Beach. He wasn't. He, his parents, and his three sisters moved here from Grove City, Florida, when Sam was in fourth grade. His sister Jenny was in fifth grade, and the twins Carol and Connie were in sixth. Sam's dad had been relocated to North Myrtle Beach for work. Sam's mom was a nurse. Sam's mom and Bree worked together for a couple of years until she retired three years ago.

The paper also said Sam had been a police officer for eight years. That was wrong. He had been with the North Myrtle Beach Police Department for eight years, but before that he was with the Surfside Police Department for three years. They were all small discrepancies, but they bothered me just the same.

When I got back to the house I scanned the yard for a newspaper. There wasn't one. When I got in the house Bree was still asleep. I decided to make myself breakfast, so I headed to the cupboard where the Pop-Tarts were kept. I scanned the boxes: Brown Sugar Cinnamon, Chocolate Fudge, Confetti Cupcake. *How can Bree eat that shit?* I wondered. I grabbed the box of blueberry Pop-Tarts, unfrosted. Opened them and put two in the toaster. I went to the Keurig and popped in a K-cup. Blueberry Mountain flavor. *Yum*, blueberry Pop-Tarts and blueberry coffee, a breakfast fit for a king.

As I sat there drinking my coffee and eating my breakfast I tried to make a go at the crossword puzzle. It was impossible to keep my mind on it. I kept looking at the clock on the microwave. I decided to give Merle a call. There was no answer. I checked my contacts for Lint and called him. Also no answer. Everyone was either busy, or just too busy to talk to me. I decided to make a trip down to the station. I left a note for Bree telling her where I had gone and that I would be back shortly.

*****

I arrived at the station and went in. It was quiet, somber. I went directly to Merle's office. He was on the phone. I took a seat on the black leather couch against the wall opposite Merle's desk. He nodded to me. I nodded back. There was a lot of stress in Merle's face. More than I had ever seen on him before.

I leaned back in the couch and looked around the room. On a short bookcase behind the desk were three trophies, two for marksmanship and one for running. Above them on the wall were medals hanging from ribbons. The medals were for marathons Merle had run. There were two diplomas on the wall behind the desk, one from Coastal Carolina, and one from the police academy. There were framed photographs around the room. There was a photograph of Merle with the mayor and one taken with the governor. A few, I didn't know who they were.

It didn't take me long to realize that Merle was talking to Sam's father. *I better call also*, I thought. Merle hung up. He stared at the phone for a few seconds before looking at me.

"How ya holding up?" he asked.

I just said, "Fine."

He nodded his head, letting me know that he understood exactly what *fine* meant.

"Any leads through the night? I asked.

Merle leaned forward, resting his forearms on the desk. "Jake, listen. You're still on vacation, and I want you to take a few extra days off. Sam was your partner. You're not taking this case, and I think you need a few extra days to process."

"Process?" I repeated the psychobabble term with distaste. "I don't need to *process* anything, Merle. What I need to do is find the bastard that killed Sam. It's obvious that Sam's murder and Helen Gere's murder are connected, and I'm sure they're connected to me in some way."

"I know, I know, the newspapers," Merle said raising his left hand to shush me.

It didn't work. "Yeah, that's right. The newspapers, *and* the dog. It's not just a coincidence that that dog was stuffed in the same newspaper box I walk to every morning. ... and there's something else. I think someone has been watching Bree and me, following us around."

Merle knitted his unruly eyebrows. "What do you mean, following you around?"

"Twice now I've seen him, once at Barefoot Landing, and then again at the beach."

"__And you didn't think you should have mentioned this before now?"

"I didn't know what to think."

Merle looked thoughtful. "What connection could the three of you possibly have? Sam was your partner I know, but what about the Gere woman? Other than questioning her once about a robbery and buying gas where she worked, what connection do you have to her?"

Merle had me there. "I don't know. What about the kid that tried to rob the place back then—, whatever happened to him?"

"That was the first thing I checked on," Lint said as he entered the room. "The kid did a year for the attempt. He was out for a while. Now he's in the middle of a two year stretch for grand theft auto." Lint sat on the edge of Merle's desk. Merle glanced over. I could tell he was thinking, *Get your fat ass off my desk, Lint*, but he didn't say anything.

I wanted to mention the Chinese place and the trail leading to Helen Gere's street, but I didn't. I didn't want Merle to know I was snooping around.

"Did you talk to her neighbors?" I asked Lint.

"Gee, great idea, Stellar. I never thought of talking to her neighbors," Lint said sarcastically, trying to do his best imitation of a complete moron. Did he not realize I had seen him do that impression every day for the last six years or so? "Of course I talked to her neighbors. I also talked to a few of Sam's neighbors this morning. No one's seen anything unusual."

"I'm just asking, Lint."

"Yeah, Stellar, well I don't need you checking on my police work. I've been a cop just as long as you have. I know how to do my job," Lint said. His face was red and a vein popped out on his forehead.

"Yeah, you're a great cop, Lint," I said getting to my feet.

"What's that supposed to mean?"

"Knock it off!" Merle yelled.

"It doesn't mean anything, Lint. You're a great cop. You can't keep your partner alive for more than two days, but other than that you're a grea—"

Lint was off the desk and moving toward me before I knew what was happening. He had the front of my shirt gripped tight in his fat little fists. We both fell onto the couch. Lint's weight crushed me and forced the air out of my lungs. I pushed forward with all of my strength and we both rolled onto the floor, me on top of Lint. I pushed away from him with the palm of my left hand on his chest and drew back my right to throw a punch into his chubby red face. Merle was behind me. He grabbed my arm before I could swing. Lint took the opportunity and let go of my shirt. He quickly doubled up his fist and connected with my jaw. It wasn't the hardest I had ever been hit but it hurt.

By this time two more officers had entered the room. One was pulling me backwards and the other was dragging Lint out from under me. We both got to our feet. Merle was between us both arms extended.

"That's enough! Jake, go home. *Now!*" he yelled. He sounded like my dad. It's funny how that tone of voice gets your attention no matter how old you are. "Lint, I'm sure you have something better to do."

"Like catching Sam's killer," I yelled, jabbing my finger in his face. Lint moved toward me again. Merle pushed him back.

"Get the hell out of here, Jake," Merle hollered.

"I'm going, I'm going," I replied, straightening my shirt as I went through the door. I rubbed the back of my head where it hit the wall and instinctively looked at my finger tips for blood. Of course there wasn't any.

Chapter Nineteen

On the way home from the station I drove by Helen Gere's house. As I took a right off of Bamwell onto First I could see Orville watering his flowers in his front lawn. He stood with a slight stoop. A lime green garden hose ran through his left hand to a shiny metal nozzle in his right. Only his arm moved as he sprayed the water back and forth across the plants. He was wearing the same tan shorts and beige short sleeve button up shirt he was wearing the other day. Or maybe that was just his retired old man uniform. I remember when I was a kid it always seemed like my grandfather wore the same thing every day. Then one day while snooping around in his closet I saw that he had about three or four pairs of the same pants; same for his shirts. From that point on we called it grandpa's uniform.

I waved to Orville. He raised the nozzle to wave back. I wondered if he remembered me or if he was just waving out of politeness.

I pulled my truck to the side of the street and got out. I walked over to the wooded path and looked around. No cigarette butts. I kicked the pine needles around with the toe of my shoe. Whoever left the butts had no reason to come back after Helen was dead. I don't really know what I was expecting to find. I turned and walked back to my truck.

"Hey, Rockford," I heard a voice call out. It was Orville.

"Stellar," I yelled back.

"I know," he shot back with a rattling laugh.

Smoker. Menthol? I wondered. *You didn't kill Helen, did ya, Orville?* I climbed back in my truck and left.

I figured I might as well drive by Sam's place. I took a right off of Eighth onto Jordan and came to a stop in front of Sam's house. I sat there with my hands on the wheel for a while just staring at Sam's. The same yellow tape that decorated Helen's door was now also guarding the entrance to Sam's.

I got out of the truck and, after trying Sam's front door and finding it locked, and finding that someone had not put the hidden key back in its place, I walked a few yards up the street looking at each home. I wondered if Sam's neighbors knew him very well. He had never talked about them. I wondered if they ever talked about him. Before yesterday, I mean.

I looked across the street at the wooded area that separated Jordan Street from the elementary school. I thought about the woods across the street from Helen's and decided that it was a good day to take a walk in the woods. I entered directly across from Sam's neighbor's house.

I walked about thirty yards and exited the trees between a swing set and basketball courts. I stopped and looked around. I turned to my left and went back into the trees. This section of trees was deeper. I walked about a hundred yards and stopped a few feet short of someone's backyard. I went to my left back toward Jordan Street. Just before reaching the street I found what I was looking for. Seven cigarette butts. "Marlboro" they said on the filter, in green letters. I got down on one knee and picked them up.

When I got back to my feet I took two steps back and side-stepped to my left behind a tree. I stood there for about five or six minutes, staring at Sam's front door. I could see every window in the front of the house, as well as the garage door and entire driveway.

The questions came in a flood: *This is where he hid in the darkness and watched Sam. How many days did he watch him? How long did it take to figure out Sam's schedule? Did he knock on the door after Sam arrived or did he run across the street and into the garage before the door closed? Did he hide in the garage or did he run right up to the car window and shoot? Did Sam order Chinese food?*

When I got back to my truck I pulled two evidence bags out of my glove compartment. I placed the butts I found at Sam's in one bag and with a Sharpie wrote SAM'S HOUSE on the bag. I took the other butts out of the ashtray and put them in the second bag and marked it HELEN'S HOUSE.

I drove home.

Chapter Twenty

"How ya doin'?" Bree asked.

"Please stop asking me how I'm doing," I shot back, probably a little too quick, too loud, and too irately.

She looked away. "Sorry. I just meant in general."

She put the pen she was holding down on the newspaper. I moved toward her as she got up. I grabbed her hand. "Sorry," I said. I pulled her toward me and put my arms round her and she laid her head on my shoulder.

"Some vacation, huh?" I asked.

"Not the best."

I squeezed her tight and kissed her head. "Did you eat?" I asked.

"I had a piece of toast. You?"

"A couple of Pop-Tarts."

"Are you hungry?"

"I could eat."

Bree said, "Let me change into something else," and headed down the hallway.

"Do you have to take a shower and do your hair?" I asked.

She stopped and turned. "What's wrong with my hair?"

Oh crap. "Nothing. I just asked."

"Does it look that bad?"

"No. It looks fine."

"Fine?"

Oh, crap. "It looks good. It *always* looks good. That's why I can't tell if you already did it or not."

"Good save," she said, turning and finishing her trek down the hall.

Whew, that was a good save.

I watched Bree's ass until she turned into our bedroom and then mentally high fived the guy that invented yoga pants. I assume it was a guy.

When she returned she was wearing white shorts and a dark blue top with very thin straps and ruffles just under her breasts. Her bra straps were showing but they were also blue.

"Belt or no belt?" she asked.

I picked *no belt* because she didn't already have a belt on. Had she been wearing a belt I would have said *belt*. I hadn't noticed the thin black belt rolled up in her left hand.

"I thought it looked better with a belt," she said.

"Then wear a belt."

"You said it looked better without one."

Oh, crap. "I didn't see the belt on you yet."

She put the belt on. I said, "That does look better."

"I thought so," she replied. "Do you think I need a sweater?"

"Yes."

*****

We decided on the Plantation Pancake House for breakfast, and we decided to walk. We walked down Hillside to Twentieth, and up Twentieth to the pancake house. As I reached for the front door I instantly regretted choosing the pancake house. Everyone in here knew us. We had been coming here for years. They also knew Sam and had probably heard the news by now. I didn't feel like being grilled about it. I took my hand off the door and looked up and down Kings Highway. I was wishing there was someplace else close by where we could be anonymous.

"What's the matter?" Bree asked.

I grabbed the door and pulled it open. "Nothing," I answered and held the door open for her.

"You go in first," she requested. So I did, and she followed.

"Well, hello there, Mr. and Mrs. Stellar," said Millie, the hostess.

Millie wore khaki pants and a Hawaiian shirt just like the waitresses. She was tall and thin and had long brown hair. She had dark eyes and thin dark eyebrows. Millie had freckles on her cheeks and a deep Southern accent. I don't know Millie's exact age but she is far too young to be named Millie. The name has always suggested old women sitting around in shawls and reeking of mothballs.

In the years we had been coming here we learned that Millie was originally from Leesburg, Georgia. We knew that she came to the Grand Strand to attend college. We knew she dropped out after the first semester. We knew she was married and we knew she had a child.

"Good morning, Millie," Bree said with a big smile.

"Good mawnin', Bree. How are y'all today?"

"We-uns is fine," I quipped.

"Kiss my grits, sugar," replied Millie good-naturedly.

She led us to a table in the middle of the dining room.

"Could we sit over here?" I said, motioning toward a booth by the front window.

Millie winked. "Sure can."

Bree ordered a mushroom and cheese omelet with hash browns and white toast. I ordered two eggs over medium with hash browns and rye toast. We both got coffee and orange juice. Our waitress was Lexie this morning. She was new. On most mornings I would have picked on the new girl, but I wasn't in the mood, so I kept my mouth shut.

Bree looked around the dining room. "It's funny, everyone that works here knows us. Do you think anyone knows us from when we used to come in here while we were on vacation, or do you think they only know us from living here?"

"I've wondered that same thing myself on occasion."

"Ricky ate here with us probably five or six times while we were on vacation different years, but I always wonder if anyone here remembers him."

"I don't know. That was more than thirteen years ago. How many of these people even worked here then?" I reached across the table and took Bree's hand.

Bree grew pensive. I saw the pupils in her eyes dilate. "Yeah, you're right. It's just sad that we live in a place where no one ever knew he existed. No one knew him. No one misses him. It bugs me sometimes. Sometimes I'll want to tell a story about him or tell someone something funny he said once, but then I'll think this person never knew him, never knew he even existed. He's buried a thousand miles away. All by himself."

The sadness in Bree's eyes when she talked about Ricky was unbearable. I sipped my coffee and rubbed her hand. I didn't know what to say. I waited for the moment to pass.

"I love you," I said.

She smiled. "I love you too."

*****

I pulled a small cigar and lighter from the side pocket of my cargo shorts and smoked it on our walk home. We held hands all the way. We didn't talk much. We walked through the back parking lot, down Madison to Twenty-Fifth and home. As we walked by the house, something in the driveway caught Bree's attention. It was a newspaper. I instantly felt a knot in my stomach. Bree started toward the paper. I knew I had to get to it before her.

"Hey, look, another paper," I said, moving in front of her. I sped up a little and bent to pick it up. I kept it folded and stuck it under my arm.

"I better call the newspaper office and let them know that we're not supposed to be getting one," Bree said.

"I'll call," I said.

When we got inside, I asked Bree if she wanted to go down to the beach for a while. She said yes and went to change. I used the opportunity to hide the newspaper in the garage and then go outside and take a look around. I walked around the house quickly and then walked around the shed. Our shed sits on the Hillside Drive side of the house in some small trees and bushes. I walked between the bushes and looked around at the ground. I found just what I thought I would. Cigarette butts, the same cigarette butts that were at Sam's and Helen's. I left the butts where they lay and went back in the house.

I felt sick to my stomach thinking that someone, a murderer, had crouched in those bushes watching us. How long had they watched us? Why were they watching us? Was I next? Was Bree next?

I wanted to go back to the garage and take a look at the paper but Bree was already in her bikini and ready to go to the beach.

I couldn't tell Bree about the cigarette butts and I hadn't told Merle about the other ones. I wanted to head over to the station but I didn't want Bree left alone and I sure didn't want her going down to the beach alone.

I decided to go to the beach with her for a while and then get her to come along with me later to the station.

Chapter Twenty-One

We pulled into the parking lot, and I asked Bree if she wanted to come in with me. She said she would wait in the truck. "Leave the keys so I can listen to the radio," she said.

I went directly to Merle's office. Lint got up from his desk and followed me. Lint leaned against the door jamb. I dropped the two baggies on Merle's desk.

"For Chrissake, Stellar, what now?" was the captains response. The response I expected.

At least there was no coffee to be spilled this time.

"Cigarette butts," I said.

"I know they're cigarette butts," Merle growled. "You should probably stick with newspaper delivery."

"Yeah," Lint said, chuckling. "Paperboy sounds a lot better than butt boy, Stellar."

I grimaced. "Good one, Lint."

"Get out, Lint," Merle said in a menacing whisper.

"But captain—," Lint complained.

"Did he just call you, Butt-Captain?" I asked.

Merle's face was fire hydrant red. "Get out! And close the door."

Lint did as he was ordered.

"So what is this about, Jake?" Merle asked.

"I found these cigarette butts on a wooded path across the street from Helen Gere's house, and the other ones I found across the street from Sam's house."

"Goddammit, Jake why did—"

"I know, I know I should have said something before, but I found the ones at Gere's and I didn't know if they meant anything. I just found the other ones yesterday at Sam's."

Merle leaned back in his chair and ran his fingers through his hair. He let out a big sigh. "Is there anything else, Jake?"

"I found some of the same butts in some bushes at the edge of my yard."

"Shit! Where's Bree?"

"She's in the truck in the parking lot. I didn't want to leave her home alone."

"Probably a good idea. What did she have to say about all of this?"

"I haven't told her."

"What?"

"I didn't want to upset her. I figured the less she knew the better."

Merle shook his head. "Maybe."

"Oh yeah, and there was another newspaper in my driveway this morning," I said.

"Where is it?" Merle scanned his desk knowing full well the newspaper wasn't there."

"In my garage. I didn't want to bring it. I didn't want Bree asking questions."

"Good idea, Jake. From now on we'll just store any murder evidence in your garage," Merle said sarcastically. "I'm gonna put a unit on your house, Jake, so you're going to have to tell Bree something."

"I'll think of something … and I'll bring that newspaper over later today."

I was almost out the door when Merle said, "Jake … Sam's … ah, Sam's wake is tomorrow night at six. His funeral is Tuesday morning."

I turned back, "Yeah, thanks, Merle. We better have plain clothes walking through the crowd. And we should probably get video of everything, just in case."

"Already on it, Jake. Go home, try to get some rest."

I shook my head and started out the door. I paused. "What about Helen Gere?"

"What about her?"

"When is her funeral? We should probably take the same precautions, just in case."

I could tell Merle didn't like his toes being stepped on, but he kept an even keel. "That's the plan, Jake, but I haven't heard anything about her funeral yet. Her daughter in Wilmington was notified the morning we found her, but they haven't been able to contact her daughter up north. I'll let you know if I hear anything."

"Yeah, Merle, keep me posted. Thanks."

*****

I opened the truck door to the sounds of Rihanna dragging her nails across a chalk board, or perhaps killing a cat. I wasn't sure.

"How can you listen to this shit?" I asked Bree.

"I like the beat," she proclaimed.

"They're all the *same* beat."

"I like it."

"I don't," I said, tapping the button marked CD. Steve Tolliver began singing "Backyard Paradise." "Now *that's* music." I sang along as I backed out of a parking space.

"You don't think all of your precious trop-rock... country... whatever songs all sound alike?" Bree asked in a snotty little tone.

"Maybe to you and Rihanna," I answered.

Chapter Twenty-Two

On our way home from the station we stopped by Hardees and grabbed take-out. I told Bree about Sam's wake and funeral the following day. I didn't tell her there would be a unit parked out front for the next few days, but when we arrived home it was sitting there. I wondered if she would notice.

"Why is that patrol car sitting there?" she asked.

I wondered if I should say "What patrol car?" Probably not.

"Merle wants one parked out front for a while. Just as a precautionary measure," I answered. "Did you want to eat in the house or on the patio?"

"Precaution to what?"

"Just because of what happened to Sam. House... patio?" I asked again.

"Is there one outside of every cop's house?"

"Soooo ... patio then?"

"Jake, what's going on?"

"Sam was my partner. They just want to make sure we're safe." I hit the button on my visor and closed the garage door behind us.

"Safe from what, Jake? What are you not telling me?" Bree asked.

I placed the bag of take-out on the kitchen table and Bree set the drinks down next to it. She went to the cupboard to grab plates and I went to the fridge to grab the ketchup, the condiment of the gods. I slathered it on everything. I'd slather it on Bree ... if she'd let me. Tonight, I'd just settle for just slathering it on the fries.

"It's those newspapers, Bree. Those three newspapers were put there on purpose, put there for me to find," I said as I walked to the garage to get the paper I had hidden. I walked back and set it on the table. I pointed to the headline about Sam. "See, it's circled, just like the other two papers, and look, there's a number four in the middle of the circle. Helen Gere was number two and the dog was number three. The dog was Helen's."

Bree stared at the papers and then asked the obvious. "Who was number one?"

"We don't know, but Merle wants the car out front to make sure you or I aren't number five." *Maybe that was too much information*, I thought.

*****

After we ate we went for a swim and sat by the pool. Around four-thirty I heard a car out front and looked over the fence. It was another patrol car pulling up. He parked behind the first unit and got out. It was Gary; he was here to relieve the other officer. *Now I feel safe. The reincarnation of Barney Fife has arrived.* The officer sped away and Gary walked back to his car. He looked over and waived.

"Hey, Jake," he yelled with a big grin.

I waved and yelled back, "Hey, Gary." *He would make a great undercover cop.* I walked back and took my seat by the pool and sipped on my ginger-ale.

"Gary?" Bree asked.

"New guy," I answered.

Chapter Twenty-Three

Believe it or not, I wasn't sleeping any better knowing Gary was sitting in a patrol car out front of my house all night. The last time I looked at the clock it was 12:38. At 3:17 I was awaken by Bree shaking my arm.

"Jake... Jake," she whispered. "I heard something."

I emerged groggily from my sleep fog. "Whazza? Something like what?"

"Like a thud," she replied. "Like someone knocked on the door."

I rubbed my eyes and leaned up on my elbows. "Someone knocked on the door?"

"No, it was just one thud."

"Why are you whispering?"

"Jake, just go check"

"Check what?"

"Jake, please. Stop joking around."

"I'll go check on Gary," I groaned.

I got out of bed and walked toward the hall.

"Aren't you going to take your gun with you?" Bree asked.

"Thuds aren't in season," I answered as I made my way into the hall. I flipped on the hall light and then did the same in the kitchen. I walked over to the widow that looked out onto Hillside. Gary was at his post. *That little bastard is sound asleep.* I turned on the coffee pot and went back to the bedroom to put on my house shoes.

Bree was sitting up in bed, the sheet pulled up to her neck. "What are you doing?"

"Gary is sound asleep in the squad car. I think I'll go out and bring him a cup of coffee."

When I got back to the kitchen I grabbed a coffee mug and filled it with hot coffee. I walked to the kitchen door and opened it.

"Jesus Christ!" I yelled, stumbling backwards and pouring hot coffee down the front of me as I tumbled to the floor. The coffee cup shattered on the ceramic tile. I quickly got to my feet and to the door. The door had swung shut. I pulled it open.

Gary's hat was stuck to the door with a large knife. Blood dripped from the knife and hat. I ran to the squad car.

Gary wasn't asleep … but he wasn't awake.

I spun around. I felt for my gun. *Shit!*

I ran as fast as I could back to the house. Bree was in the kitchen. Her hands were pressed to her heaving chest.

"What's the matter, Jake? What happened?" she asked in a loud whisper.

I flew by her to the bedroom and to the night stand. I yanked open the drawer and pulled out my gun. "Bree," I yelled, "get back here!"

"What's the matter?"

"Get back here *right now!*" I shouted.

She ran into the bedroom. "Dammit, Jake, wha—"

I grabbed her by the wrist and pulled her to the closet door. I opened the door and forced her into the closet and onto the floor.

"Stay there, don't move!" I shouted. "Don't open this door until I come back for you."

She was crying. She nodded her head. I shut the door.

I ran back to Gary's squad car. I was barefoot now, having stumbled out of my house shoes.

I placed my index and middle fingers on Gary's neck. His neck was sticky from the blood. There was a faint heartbeat. Gary opened his eyes for just a second, looked up at me, and then closed his eyes again. I pulled my T-shirt off over my head and put it on Gary's throat and applied pressure. I could feel my shirt getting wet. I let go of his throat and hit the button to unlock the doors and then ran around to the passenger side. I opened the door and grabbed the radio mic.

"Officer down, officer down!" I yelled. "This is Detective Stellar, I need an ambulance and backup at two five zero two Hillside Drive. I repeat, officer down! Two five zero two Hillside drive."

"Copy that," came the dispatcher's voice over the radio.

I threw the mic on to the seat and ran back to Gary a put the T-shirt back on his throat. I felt for a pulse again but couldn't feel anything. "Hang on, Gary, hang on. Help is on the way."

I could hear a slight panic in the female dispatcher's voice as she called for units in the area.

I knew only seconds had passed but it seemed like an eternity. "God dammit!" I screamed. Then I heard sirens. "They're almost here, Gary. Hang on."

Gary's blood had soaked the shirt and was now seeping between my fingers. I laid my forehead against the cool steel of the roof, my arm dangling at my side. I waited. The sirens got louder.

Chapter Twenty-Four

Gary died at around three 3:25 that Monday morning with my shirt wrapped around the gash in his throat. The look in his eyes when he opened them and looked at me will haunt me for the rest of my life. There was fear in his eyes, and I wondered if he saw the fear in *my* eyes. I wondered if he felt safe knowing I had found him. I wondered if he even saw me.

Bree and I sat at the kitchen table with Merle and Lint. Lint asked most of the questions. He didn't seem like as big of an ass hole as usual. His questions were slow but to the point. His voice was soft and for once he didn't ask or say anything stupid. Merle didn't say much.

Crime Scene was all over our yard and house. I had showed them where I had found and left the cigarette butts. They had dusted the knife and Gary's hat for prints while it still hung on our front door. They found no prints on either.

Chavez, one of the investigators with Crime Scene, pulled the knife from the door with his gloved hand, holding Gary's hat with the other. He placed the knife in an evidence bag that was being held by another investigator. Chavez turned the hat over and looked inside.

"Captain, you better have a look at this," Chavez said, pulling a piece of white paper form inside the sweatband of the hat. He unfolded the paper. "It's a note." Chavez looked at me. "To Jake."

Merle got up from the table. An officer handed him a pair of latex gloves. Merle put them on and took the note.

How does it feel Jake? How does it feel to

lose people you care about? How does it feel to

watch them die around you? A man could

lose his sanity. Who's next, Jake?

Who's next?

Your past

Merle walked over and handed me the note. I read it to myself. *What did it mean?*

"Do you recognize the handwriting?" Lint asked.

There's the Lint I've come to know. I glared at him over the top of the note but didn't answer. I looked back down and read it again. I handed the note back to Merle. He handed it back to Chavez, who put it in an evidence bag.

Merle turned back to me. "I guess this is about you after all."

I cringed.

Bree approached, her eyes wild with fear. "What do you mean, *about Jake*? And what do you mean, *after all*?"

Merle knew he had slipped up just as the words left his mouth, but he wasn't about to help me out from underneath the bus where he had thrown me. He simply turned around and headed for the door, saying, "Looks like you two have some things to discuss. I'm going to have another unit sit on your house 24/7 till this thing is over, Jake. Two officers this time."

"What do we have to discuss, Jake?" Bree asked. Her voice could have cut glass. *"What do we have to discuss?"*

Lint got up from the table and followed Merle. Bree went to the bedroom. I followed. Bree walked through the bedroom door and slammed it behind her. *Oh, crap.* I paused at the door, and then went in.

Bree was already sitting at the foot of the bed.

Where to start? "Bree, I'm sorry. I just thought it was better to keep some things to my se—" My phone rang. I pulled it from my pocket and looked at the number. Didn't recognize it. Answered it anyway. "Hello?"

"Jake Stellar?" asked a woman's voice.

"It's Kim … Kim Lee."

"Kim Lee?" I asked, puzzled.

"From the Hong Kong Restaurant. You gave me your card the other day. You told me to call you if anything came up."

"Yes, I remember. What is it, Miss Lee?"

"The other day you asked me if anyone had quit recently."

"Yeah?"

"Well, a young man who works here, he delivers sometimes, Tommy Chen. He was supposed to work yesterday. He called in sick. He was supposed to work again today but he never showed up. I called his house a few times this morning but his mother said he never came home last night."

"Can you give me his address and phone number, Miss Lee?"

"Yes."

I wrote Tommy Chen's name, address, and phone number on a note pad on the night stand.

"I gotta go," I said to Bree, and kissed her on the forehead. "I love you. We'll talk when I get back."

I quickly explained everything to the officers that were left at the house and told them to sit tight and stay alert that we got a lead on a guy and his whereabouts were unknown. I told one of the officers to stay in the house with Bree.

On the way to the station I phoned Merle and filled him in on my call from Kim Lee. I read off Tommy Chen's phone number and address and told Merle I would be there in a few seconds.

When I arrived at the station, Merle was in the briefing room with a dozen or so officers, a mixture of uniforms and plain clothes. Merle was standing at a small podium that sat on a desk, addressing the group.

"Forensics matched fingerprints found in the Gere home with Tommy Chen, a known felon," the captain was saying. "Chen is probably armed. And we know he is dangerous. He has three priors: one for robbery and two for assault. He was arrested once for assaulting his mother and once for assaulting his girlfriend. Earlier we had an officer call his mother's house pretending to be a friend of Chen's. His mother told the officer that Chen was at his girlfriend's apartment. He is still dating the same girl he assaulted. We have her address on file. Are there any questions?"

"Does he know karate?" Lint asked.

Merle shook his head. "Are there any *intelligent* question?"

Lint looked around the room and shrugged his shoulders.

Chapter Twenty-Five

We rolled up to Chen's girlfriend's apartment in three white unmarked vans with tinted windows, no lights, no sirens. The apartment was a small duplex that appeared to have been a single family home at one time. The apartment Chen was in was downstairs.

One van rolled in from the north. One parked on the street behind the apartment and the van I was in pulled up from the south. The officers behind the house exited their van first and moved cautiously through the neighbor's backyard and into the apartment building's backyard. A few seconds later the doors of the other two vans opened and the rest of us moved in.

Merle, Lint and I were at the front door, our guns drawn at our sides. Other officers were beside and below windows. Their guns were also drawn. I knocked.

"Tommy Chen!" I yelled through the door. "North Myrtle Beach Police Department."

Lint hit the door with the battering ram and stepped aside. I was first in followed by Merle. A very large Caucasian woman was standing in the middle of the living room. She started to run toward the back door just as it was kicked in by another officer.

"Get down!" I yelled. She froze and threw her hands in the air.

"Don't shoot me, don't shoot me!" she yelled.

Merle grabbed her by the back of her shirt and forced her to the floor. I heard glass break from another room and quickly made my way down the hall toward the sound. I held my GLOCK G30S in a white-knuckle grip.

I looked in the bathroom and yelled, "Secure!"

Another officer secured a bedroom. I went to the second bedroom. There was yelling coming from outside. I went into the bedroom. The window had been smashed out. I walked to the window and looked out. Tommy Chen was face down on the lawn. An officer had a knee in Chen's back and was placing handcuffs on his wrists. I let out a deep breath that I didn't know I was holding.

As I walked back through the living room I looked in an ashtray on an end table. In the ashtray were several cigarette butts, Marlboro, menthol.

Chapter Twenty-Six

As I got to the door of the interrogation room, Merle was walking out. He closed the door behind him. He was carrying a file folder. I held my hand out and he gave it to me. I opened it and flipped through its contents. It contained the usual: graphic pictures of the deceased to shake up the douche in custody, get him off his game. There was also the finger print findings, a list of the stolen goods, the girlfriend's statement, Chen's work schedule from the restaurant, and a few take-out menus, as well as some blank pages just to bulk up the file.

Through a window in the hall I could see Chen sitting in a metal folding chair at a white, six-foot-long banquet table. He was handcuffed to a small bar that was bolted to the table. The room was painted white and the lighting was very bright and the air condition vent was closed. It was not a comfortable room. We didn't want it to be.

"Do you know this guy?" Merle asked.

"Never seen him before in my life," I responded. "Why, did he say he knew me?"

"No, but the note said, 'your past.'"

"Maybe his father?"

"No father. The mother said the kid's father took off a couple weeks after he was born. They haven't seen him since."

Lint came down the hall toward us. "Get anything?"

"Nothing," Merle answered.

"Search warrant at his mother's turn up anything?" I asked.

"Sure did," Lint said. "We found a small safe that had been busted open. We found a bunch of jewelry, rings, necklaces things like that. There's a list of everything in the file. Chen's girlfriend was wearing a necklace and some ear rings that she said Chen gave her on Wednesday. She said he's had a lot of cash on him the last couple days. We found some old war medals. Gere's daughter is driving over to identify the stuff, but we're sure it's Gere's."

"The girlfriend still here?" I asked.

Merle said, "No. we cut her loose, told her we would be in contact."

I put my hand on the door knob.

"Where do you think you're going?" Lint asked snottily

My answer was remarkably even, given that I wanted to kick him in the nuts. "I'm going in to talk to Chen."

"Do I need to remind you again that this is my case, Stellar?"

"Do I need to remind you that you're one fat bas—"

"Jake!" Merle said. "Lint, give him a few minutes with Chen."

Lint rolled his eyes and stomped down the hall toward the vending machine.

I raised the file folder. "You show the pictures to Chen?" I asked Merle.

"No. Be my guest."

I went in and shut the door behind me. I glanced up at the video camera mounted in the corner facing Chen. Chen followed my lead and also looked toward the camera. I turned to the window that separated the hallway from the interrogation room and closed the mini blinds. I tossed the file on the table and sat down.

"Ya know, before they installed that camera I averaged about twenty-five minutes per confession," I began. "After they installed it, about forty-five minutes."

I looked at my watch for effect. Tommy Chen sat silently. He slouched back in his chair and even managed an insolent grin. But I saw his lip quiver. I could see it in his eyes: he was scared. I lifted the file and opened it.

"Let's see here, you killed an old woman and two cops. That's lethal injection, Tommy. No way around it. They're gonna strap you to a table, find a vein, and th—"

"I didn't kill that old lady and I di—"

"Shut up, Tommy," I said in a don't-gimme-that-shit voice. He complied. "I didn't ask you if you killed anybody. I'm not *going* to ask you if you killed anybody. That's not why I'm here, Tommy boy. I already know you killed somebody, and I know who you killed. I'm here to find out *why* you killed somebody." I started placing the 8x10 color photos of Helen Gere, Gary Finder, and Sam

Chandler on the table in front of Chen. I didn't have a photo of the dog or I would have put that out, too.

"I want a lawyer," Tommy blurted out.

"*Shhhh,* Tommy. Not so loud. I'm going to pretend I didn't hear that. You see, you lawyer up and we have to charge you, and we're going to charge you with first-degree murder, three counts. That means they're going to try you for three different murders. Only one's gotta stick, Tommy. Now you gotta ask yourself, if there's enough evidence in this folder," I placed my hand on the closed folder, "to convince *me* that you killed someone, then how hard is it going to be for the DA, and he's a *very good* DA, to convince twelve decent, God-fearing people that a, pardon my French, skinny-assed Asian punk with a chip on his shoulder killed someone?"

By this time, Chen had lost his smart-ass grin. There were beads of sweat on his brow and his hands trembled. He went to wipe away the sweat, forgetting that his hand was cuffed to the table. He winced and used the other hand.

"But I swea—"

I put my finger to my lips. "*Shhhh.*"

"Your girlfriend was more than happy to tell us about the extra cash you've had the last couple of days, and the jewelry you gave her. Mrs. Gere's daughter is on her way here now to identify the jewelry. We found your finger prints in Mrs. Gere's home. We found her husband's medals at your mom's house." I looked at Chen and slowly shook my head. "Open and shut, Tommy. Open and shut."

"She was already dead when I got th—"

"Already dead when you got there," I repeated.

The door swung open. Merle said, "His mother got him a lawyer."

I looked back at Chen. "Tommy, do you know what the number one thing a murderer says just before he confesses?"

"No."

"Already dead when I got there." I stood up from the table. Before I left the room I turned back to Chen and said, "Look on the bright side, Tommy. They probably won't charge you for killing the dog."

I recognized Chin's attorney, but didn't know him by name. He was fat and had big fat hands that made the brief case he was carrying look like it was made for a child. He had beady little eyes that were too close together, a flat nose, and thick, saggy jowls that gave him the appearance of being half man, half pig. His face was clean shaven and shiny with sweat. He looked like he had just polished off a bucket of greasy chicken all by himself. I could almost hear the sound of his lips sucking every bit of grease from his fingertips. He was wearing a moth-eaten seersucker suit that Ben Matlock wouldn't be caught dead in, that he had already managed to soak through at the back and armpits. His hair was dark black with specks of white dandruff or dry skin throughout. He waddled back and forth as he moved down the hall.

"Gentleman," he said in a cultured-sounding Low country accent, probably Charleston born and educated, as he tried to squeeze between me and the door jamb, "I would like a moment alone with my client, please." He went in and quietly shut the door behind him.

"Anything?" Merle asked.

"He said Gere was dead when he got there. We were interrupted before I got to Gary or Sam."

"Did you ask him why he has been following you, or anything about the newspapers, or your past?"

"Didn't get to any of that?" I handed the folder back to Merle. "I'm going home. I'm on vacation."

Chapter Twenty-Seven

Sam's wake was nothing like my dream. There was no open casket. There wasn't even a casket. Sam was cremated, and his ashes were in a decorative brass urn placed atop a dark mahogany table. There were racks of flowers from the floor to a height of about five feet, arranged in a semi-circle around the table. Their sickly sweet smell gave me a slight headache. The usual generic funeral home music played in the background. It offered no comfort but made my headache worse.

The receiving line consisted of Sam's mother and father, his three sisters, Jenny, Carol, and Connie, and their husbands. Carol's daughter was the only niece or nephew in the line; she stood between her mother and father. The other children sat in chairs across the room with their great grandfather.

Bree and I arrived at the funeral home early but so did a lot of other people. As the line slowly moved, we passed by a television that played a memorial video documenting Sam's life. There were photos of Sam as a child, as well as a teenage Sam in football and baseball uniforms. There were photos of Sam graduating from the police academy. The hardest photographs for me to see were the ones of Sam and me together. There was one of us on a boat; that was a great day. There was one that took place at a barbeque at my house. There was one of Bree and me and Sam and a girl he dated for a while. Gale, her name was. The four of us were seated in a booth at a restaurant. It was New Year's Eve I think. She moved away about a year ago. Her job took her out west. I looked around the room to see if she was here. I wondered if she even knew. Each picture made me smile but at the same time the lump in my throat was almost unbearable. I fought back tears. I kept blinking. I wanted to scratch my eye but I was afraid someone might think I was wiping away a tear. Big boys don't cry. Not in public anyway.

We made it through the line in about fifteen minutes. We said, "Sorry for your loss," several times, and shook a lot of hands and gave out a lot of hugs. Sam's mother and father seemed to be holding up well; his sisters did not. His niece looked like a deer caught in the headlights.

Bree and I made our way to another room where several police officers and their wives had staked a claim. Bree gravitated to the wives and hugged a few. I shook the hands of the men I knew and nodded to the ones I didn't. None of us said, "How are you doin'?" or "Sorry for your loss." Among the cops I knew such meaningless pleasantries were frowned upon. We bore up under our stress and grief stoically. Wonder what my pinheaded shrink would have said about *that*?

"Chen still ain't talking," Chavez said.

"That's what I heard," I answered.

"Someone said you have a history with this guy?" Gwen asked.

"Not that I know of," I answered. "I don't think I've ever seen this kid before in my life."

Another officer said, "I hope the bastard ge—" He stopped abruptly and walked away.

Lint said, "The note says 'from your past.' What do you think that means?"

Surprise, surprise, he wasn't being a dick. "I have no idea. I wish I could have questioned him just a little bit longer."

"Well the DA will be asking all the questions from this point on," Chavez chimed in. "They booked him on murder one. Gere's daughter identified the jewelry this afternoon. We have robbery for a motive. We have opportunity, and we can place Chen in the house."

"But why Sam and Gary?" I asked. "And what is his connection to me?"

"Who knows?" Lint interjected, pulling a large silver flask out of his jacket pocket. He removed the cap, took a big swig and passed it to Chavez. Chavez passed it to Gwen. My mouth watered. Gwen started to pass it to me but hesitated and passed it back to Lint, who took one more swig and placed it back in his pocket. He adjusted his jacket.

"Any word on the Gere funeral?" I asked.

Chavez said, "They still haven't located the older daughter. I guess they've put out a missing person bulletin on her. She hasn't shown up for work in over a week. Friends or family haven't heard from her either."

"Lives up north somewhere, doesn't she?" Gwen asked.

Chavez again: "Yeah. New York City, I guess. She's a nurse at Bellevue," Chavez answered.

"Bellevue, isn't that some big nut house or something?" Lint asked.

"Or something," Chavez answered. His expression made it clear he thought Lint had shit for brains.

The women kept giving us the evil eye for talking shop at the funeral so we changed the topic of conversation to baseball. Me being the only Yankee fan in the room made it a pretty one-sided discussion.

Around eight-thirty the crowd at the funeral home began to thin. We went over to Sam's family and told them good-bye. We gave a few last hugs and handshakes and made our way toward the door.

A few of the guys and their wives decided to reconvene at a small bar around the corner from the funeral home. Bree and I declined and went home instead.

On the way home Bree let me know that she needed a drink. I kept the fact that I needed one, too, to myself.

"We could have gone to the bar with the others if you wanted to," I said.

"No, I didn't want to go. I'm tired. Can we just run in Bi-Lo and grab a six pack?"

"Sure."

Bree grabbed a six pack of Michelob Ultra. I knew I had ginger-ale at home so I just grabbed a bag of potato chips and some French onion dip.

We sat on the couch, flipping through the channels and munching on our chips until around eleven o'clock, when Bree said, "We better get to bed. We have a long day ahead of us tomorrow."

I agreed and followed her to bed. For once in my eternally horny life, the thought of hanky-panky was the furthest from my mind.

Chapter Twenty-Eight

Tuesday morning was beautiful. We had slept with the bedroom window open. I could hear the birds chirping before I ever opened my eyes. The sun shined through the window, and I could feel its warmth on my legs through the bedspread. Bree was already up, and I could hear morning show talking heads blathering on the TV in the living room. She walked in with a cup of coffee and placed it on the night stand.

"Thank you," I said.

"You're most welcome, Highness," she responded.

Bree was already dressed in her running clothes. I stretched my arms toward the ceiling and yawned loudly.

"You want to go for a run?" Bree asked.

"I'm *way* too comfortable." I reached over and took a sip of my coffee. *Ahh, blueberry.*

"I'm going to go by myself then."

"You want to grab a paper on your way back?" I asked.

"Sure."

"I'll get you some change." I got out of bed and went to the change dish that sat on my dresser. "Are you sure you wouldn't rather climb back and bed and get a little *horizontal* exercise?"

Bree flexed her eyebrows, Groucho-style. "How about when I get back? I'm only going to go a couple miles."

"It's a date," I said. *Score!*

Bree took the change from me and put it in her pocket. I heard it jingle. *That's gonna drive her nuts.* Then she grabbed her cell phone off of her nightstand and put that in her other pocket, and went out the door.

I picked up my coffee and went to the kitchen window to see if I could catch her stretching in the driveway before her run. Watching Bree stretch is like runner's porn. By the time I got to the window she was half way down the street. *Crap.*

As I looked out the window, I saw a newspaper lying on the lawn. My stomach dropped and every hair on my body stood instantly on end. *Gary's newspaper,* I thought. *Gary is number five, but how? Chen is in jail.* I ran out into the yard and picked up the paper. I opened it. It wasn't the *Sun News*. It was a copy of Monday's *New York Times*. I set it on the kitchen table and flipped through the pages. On one of the back pages of the A section was a headline that read BELLEVUE NURSE STILL MISSING. The headline was circled and in the middle of the circle was the number one. *Bellevue. Son of a bitch.*

I ran to the bedroom and quickly got dressed, grabbed my truck keys, and went out the door to find Bree.

I drove down Hillside as far as I thought she might have gotten, then I took a right on Fifteenth. I slowly drove down to Ocean Boulevard, looking up and down each street I crossed. When I got to Ocean Boulevard I stopped and looked both ways. She said she was only going a couple miles, so I pulled into the Jamaica Inn's parking lot. I got out of my truck and ran down the access path to the beach. She was nowhere in sight. An elderly man and woman were walking their dog along the beach.

"Excuse me," I said, "did you see a woman run by here? She's about five-four, reddish brown hair. She had on black shorts, a white T-shirt, and pink and white running shoes."

"Only two people ran by us, they were both men. We just came out here," the man answered, pointing toward their hotel.

"Thank you," I said and ran back to my truck.

I decided to drive back toward the house while calling Merle's cell phone.

"Hello," Merle said.

"Merle, its Jake. There was another newspaper this morning,"

"Another newspa—"

"Listen, Merle," I could feel myself becoming frantic. "The newspaper it was a copy of the *New York Times*."

"*New York Times*? Why, what does tha—"

"In the paper there's an article about Gere's daughter being missing. There's a circle around the headline with the number one inside it," I said. My heart felt like it was going to burst through my chest. I was talking a mile a minute and wondering if Merle could even understand me.

"Gere's daughter is number one? How can that be?" Merle asked. "Chen, he was in holding all night."

"Merle, Bree went for a run this morning. I can't find her. I'm in my truck headed back toward my house."

"I'll put out a missing persons immediately. What was she wearing?"

I described her clothing to Merle and hung up just as I arrived at home. I leapt from the truck and went into the house.

"Bree! Bree!" I called out several times. I ran to the bathroom and then to the pool. She wasn't there. My heart was pounding faster. There was a numbness in my hands and face. I couldn't get a deep breath. My phone rang. The readout said it was Bree. *Thank God.* I answered.

"Bree—,"

"Jake Stellar," came a man's voice from the other end. "I assume this is Jake Stellar. You were listed as 'hubby' in the contacts."

"Who is this?" I asked. My voice was shaky.

"Hubby. That's nice. I like nicknames, Jake."

"Who is this? What do you want?"

"I have a nickname for your lovely wife, Jake. Do you know what it is?"

I didn't answer.

He repeated: "Do. You. Know. What. It. Is ... Jake?" Every sinisterly enunciated word was a stab to my heart.

I tried and failed to tame the tremor in my voice. "No."

"Number six."

Something in my head clicked. It suddenly all made sense. "I swear to God, Mason, if you hurt her, I'll fucking kill you!" I screamed into the phone.

"So, you finally figured it out, Jake. It took you long enough. I thought for sure you would figure it out when you read the note I left you. I mean, after all, how many people do you know who would want to watch you lose every one you care about? My guess would have been, just the one person you did the same thing to. You took everything from me, Jake."

I tried to calm down. "Mason, it wasn't my fault. It was an accident. I lost my son, too."

"You don't get it, do you Jake?" He was hysterical. "I lost everyone, everyone I cared about! And now you're going to lose the one person you care about *the most*."

"Please, Mason, don't do this," I pleaded.

"Oh, don't worry, Jake, I wouldn't think of doing this without you. I want you to watch, just like I did. I'll be in touch."

The phone call ended. Several patrol cars pulled up in front of my house. I tried to call Bree's phone back. It went straight to voice mail.

Chapter Twenty-Nine

I hated feeling helpless, but at this point there was nothing for me to do but wait. My instinct told me that Bree was safe ... for now. Mason didn't want to *hurt* her, he wanted to *kill* her. He wanted to *hurt* me. And he sure knew how to go about doing that.

By now every cop in a two hundred mile radius had Bree's description and was looking for her. Every abandoned building was being searched. Every empty storefront was being searched. A photograph of Bree was being broadcast on every local TV station, as well as a photograph of Phillip Mason.

One of the tech guys had hooked up some kind of electronic device to our landline and something had also been installed on my cell. I didn't know exactly what the devices were, I didn't need to know. I wasn't that kind of cop.

The house was quiet. I had just asked everyone to leave the kitchen with the exception of Merle, who sat across from me at the kitchen table.

"So, who is this Phillip Mason, and what is his connection to you, Jake?" Merle asked.

I looked around the room to make sure no one else was within earshot. I sighed. "Where to begin?" I whispered.

"How about at the beginning."

So, I started from the beginning.

"Phillip Mason owned a small restaurant on Lydig Avenue in the Bronx. He was a husband and a father of three. He came from a good, middle-class family. He was born and raised in the Bronx. He went to culinary school and became a chef. Mason saved every dime he made for ten years and bought his own restaurant."

I paused. I hadn't thought of the name Phillip Mason in years, but I couldn't believe how much I knew about him. I sat still, my arms on the table, my fingers clasped in front of me, the memories of my encounter with Phillip Mason playing out in my head.

"Go on," Merle prompted me.

"After work one Friday night, around five, I picked up Ricky from daycare. He went there after school on the nights Bree worked. On the way home we stopped at The Mason Jar, that was the name of Mason's restaurant, for take-out. A lot of cops hung out there at that time, so I kinda knew Mason and his family. Not real well but I knew their names and faces.

He had a nice place, Merle, a nice bar, and the restaurant was small and quiet. It only sat around fifty people, but it was always full. The guy had a great life.

"So Ricky and I go in and place our order. We took a seat at the bar and we each had a soda while we waited. Kids aren't supposed to sit at the bar, but because I was a cop no one said anything. Just before our order came out, I see Mason walk out of the kitchen. He walked up to the end of the bar and asked his wife for a beer. His wife worked the bar during the day. She handed him the beer, and he stood there drinking it while the two of them chatted."

"I heard him tell his wife that he was going to have to go to the grocery store and pick up a couple of things for the restaurant before the dinner rush. She asked if he wanted her to go instead. He said no, that he wanted to get out of the place for a while. Our food came out and we left.

"When I got back to the car I noticed that I had forgotten Ricky's book bag at daycare, so I turned around and went back."

I took a deep breath. Merle was listening intently. He probably knew most of the story about Ricky's death but didn't interrupt. It was the part I was getting to that he didn't know.

"We were about half-way home from Ricky's daycare when Ricky asked me to put in one of his CDs. He said he wanted to listen to some music. Ricky was in the back seat. I reached up over the passenger side visor to retrieve the CD. As I was sliding it in the slot, I quickly glanced up at the road. The light was red, but it was too late.

"A truck broadsided us on the passenger side, the side where Ricky was sitting. The impact was so great that it caved in the rear passenger side door about three feet and shattered the windows on that side of the car. The car spun around several times. The driver's side door broke open. I wasn't wearing my seat belt and I was thrown from the car.

"It's true what they say, everything slows down. I can still remember every tumble as I rolled across the street. Every time I came around, I could see the car as it spun. I came to rest at the edge of the street against the curb. My car came to rest against a telephone pole about twenty-five yards away from me.

"I immediately jumped to my feet; it must have been the adrenaline. My arms and hands dripped blood. My pants were ripped and my leg was bleeding. I staggered toward the car. The rear driver's side door was open. I could see Ricky, hunched over and bloody. I reached across the seat and lifted his head. I knew the minute I saw the side of his head that he was dead.

"By this time patrol cars had arrived. They were all cops from my precinct. They recognized me right away. An ambulance pulled up, and then another. They pulled Ricky from the car and started working on him.

"There was a little girl lying in the street. She had gone through the windshield of the truck that hit us. I looked to the truck. I didn't recognize the truck, but I recognized the driver as the emergency workers pulled him from behind his air bag. It was Phillip Mason. He was conscious, and calling out for his little girl who lay in the street.

"My eyes went back to Ricky. One paramedic looked at the other and shook his head 'no.' He took the stethoscope out of his ear. I walked over to where Ricky laid and fell to my knees. I leaned over and put my forehead against his little chest. Tears were streaming from my eyes. I could hear Mason screaming his daughter's name. I don't know what made me do it, but I raised my head and said to the officer standing closest to me, 'Get a breathalyzer on him.'

"The officer looked at me puzzled and said, 'But … his little girl—.'

"I said, 'Do it, now.' And they did."

Merle gave a low, sad, weary whistle. "Jesus Christ."

"Yeah. Mason blew a .07 the first two attempts, but on that third try he blew a .08. The officers cuffed him and put him in the back of the squad car. He sat there in hand cuffs while his daughter lay there in the street, dying. He kept looking at me with this look on his face like he was asking me for help. Every one of those cops at the scene knew him. They had all eaten in his restaurant. They had bent elbows at his bar. But one word from me and he was nobody, he was nothing."

Merle opened his mouth to say something, but nothing came out.

I continued. "Mason was charged with two counts of involuntary manslaughter, two counts of endangering the welfare of a child, driving under the influence, and a few other things. Mason lost it. He was found not competent to stand trial, and he was sent to Bellevue. About six months later his wife put the other two kids to bed one night. After they fell asleep she took a butcher knife and slit both of their throats. Then she got into bed and put Mason's pistol against her temple and fired."

Merle sat there for what seemed like forever. I knew he was trying to justify in his own mind what I had done. He couldn't and neither could I. He leaned back in his chair and stared at the ceiling, rubbing the top of his head with his fingers. He leaned forward and put his forearms on the edge of the table and leaned in toward me like he was going to tell me some big secret.

"You didn't do anything any other grieving father wouldn't have done, Jake, in the heat of the moment, cop or no cop, "Merle said. "Your ethics aren't in question. The guy had been drinking."

"Merle, I've told myself that same lie for eleven years. But the truth is, I caused that accident. I went through the red light. Mason had had a couple of drinks. Just enough to blow the magic number. It was my fault, Merle. I killed my son. I killed that whole family, and now Bree is going to pay for what I've done."

"No, she's not." Merle picked up his coffee mug and mine, too, and went to the coffee maker. "We'll get her back, Jake." He made us each another cup of coffee and brought them back to the table.

I wrapped my hands around the coffee mug and stared inside as though the answer to my problems was going to reveal itself in the inky blackness of the steaming brew.

"Jake, this conversation never leaves this table," Merle said emphatically. "You understand me?"

I nodded my head yes.

Chavez returned to the kitchen. "Captain, everything is all set. He makes a phone call and we got him, whether he calls from a cell or a land line."

"Thanks, Chavez," Merle said. "Now we wait."

"Chavez, help yourself to the coffee," I said, motioning toward the coffee maker.

"Don't mind if I do," he returned. He made himself a cup and took a seat at the table with Merle and me. Chavez reached across the table and put his hand on my forearm, gave it a brotherly squeeze and said, "We'll get her back, Jake."

Catch-phrase of the day.

Chapter Thirty

No call came that day, or that night. Needless to say, I didn't make it to Sam's funeral. Merle did go. He said it was a nice service. That's what everyone says about every service. But they're never nice.

A surveillance team was set up at the funeral to take pictures and video of the crowd. One of Sam's sisters would probably be asked to watch the footage to point out who she didn't know and who she did know.

Along with a few other officers, I stayed at the house the entire day to answer the phone. The phone rang about six or seven times between ten and nine and everyone snapped to attention. Each time it rang it was either a telemarketer, someone wanting to save me a lot of money on my mortgage payment, or a wrong number.

At one point there was even a call from a young woman asking me if I was happy with my newspaper delivery. I explained to her that I had not recently been happy with my newspaper delivery, but that I didn't want to go into details at this time. Chavez grinned. I knew she had the wrong number but I thanked her anyway. I felt like being nice to people, what with karma and all.

Merle got back to the house around seven. Lint was there because it was his job. So was Chavez and the others, but Merle was there because he wanted to be.

There were no calls at all after nine. I didn't go to bed though. I tried watching TV a few times but couldn't keep my mind on what I was watching. Mostly Merle and I sat at the table and drank coffee. I dozed off a couple of times with my head on the table, but never for more than a few minutes. I was going bat shit crazy on the inside but I tried to stay as calm as possible on the outside.

When morning came I decided to make breakfast for the guys. Lee Parker offered to run and pick up doughnuts. I told him I would rather make breakfast. It would give me something to do; something to keep my mind off of what I knew was coming next.

I made each guy two eggs over medium with bacon and white toast, except for Lint. Lint informed me that he didn't like runny yokes. It made him want to puke. He asked if I could make him scrambled eggs instead. I did. While eating his breakfast he informed me that the bacon was too floppy, that he liked his bacon stiff. I informed him that this wasn't a restaurant, and that most of the guys and I had already heard that he liked his pork stiff. The guys laughed. I don't think Lint got it, because he just wagged his head yes.

Parker ate his breakfast in front of the television, flipping back and forth from The Jerry Springer Show to the Weather Channel to Rachael Ray. The first time I met Parker my first thought was, *Is there no height requirement for the North Myrtle Beach Police*

Department? I found it hard to believe that Puny Parker the Hobbit, as some of the crueler cops called him behind his back, was allowed on any roller coaster in any amusement park in the country, so how did he become a cop? He couldn't have been more than five-three. I soon found out that his grandfather was once the chief of police, and that his father served as a council member for eight years. That's how he probably got the job but not how he kept it. He was a good cop.

Parker was twenty-nine years old but looked seventeen. He had blond hair so sun-bleached and light that, at a distance, he looked like he had no hair at all. The same went for his eyebrows. I had never asked him, but I was sure he had never shaved a day in his life. He had chubby cheeks, like he still possessed every ounce of baby fat he had brought into this world.

"Jake, you had better come in here," Parker called out.

I walked into the living room to see a full screen picture of Bree on the television. Underneath her picture the caption read, MISSING, LOCAL NURSE, BREE ANN STELLAR. The graphic darted to the corner of the screen as the anchorwoman began talking to the camera.

"Eye-witness News has just learned that the missing North Myrtle Beach nurse whose picture has been circulating the Grand Strand and surrounding areas is the wife of North Myrtle Beach police detective Jake Stellar. Stellar, a twenty-five year police veteran and six-year North Myrtle Beach police detective, and his wife moved to the area from the Bronx in New York after the death of their son, Richard."

The picture of Bree switched to a picture of Phillip Mason.

"Eye-witness News has also learned that this man, Phillip Allen Mason, may be Mrs. Stellar's kidnapper.

"Mason, also of the Bronx, has a past history with the Stellars. Jake Stellar and Mason were involved in a car accident thirteen years ago that claimed the life of Richard Stellar, as well as the life of Mason's daughter, Abigail Mason. Both children were six years old at the time of the accident."

Parker, Lint, and Chavez were all staring at me. When I returned the stares, they looked back toward the TV. "Turn it off," I said and walked out of the room.

"We go live now to th—" Click.

There was a knock at the door. *Jesus Christ!* I looked out the kitchen window. There were two vans outside, one from WMBG, the NBC affiliate, and another from WFXB, the FOX affiliate. The satellite dishes on the roofs looked huge and ominous.

I made my way to the front door. Merle, red-faced and clearly angry held up his hand to halt me. I stopped and he went to the door and opened it.

"Jake Stellar can you comme—"

"I'm not detective Stellar," Merle replied.

"Can we please spe—"

Merle raised his hands to the reporters. "Detective Stellar will not be giving a statement at this time. Please remove yourself from the property or you will be arrested for trespassing and hindering an ongoing investigation."

"The people have the right to kn—"

Merle said, "Thank you" and shut the door. He looked to Parker. "Get some more units down here and get a secure perimeter around this house. I don't want anyone within one hundred feet of this house."

"Yes sir," said Parker. He pulled his radio off his belt and went out the door with Chavez.

"We didn't need that," I said.

Merle clapped me on the back. "No, my friend, we didn't."

Within a few minutes several squad cars, along with two SUVs, came to a stop along Hillside and Twenty Fifth Avenue. Officers immediately began setting up sawhorses and running yellow plastic caution tape between the sawhorses. Another officer began herding the reporters and onlookers, who had started to arrive in droves, behind the barrier.

I looked at the clock. It was one o'clock. Still no phone call.

Chavez and Parker reentered the house. "We didn't need this," Parker said.

"No, we didn't," Merle and I answered together.

My cell phone rang. I picked it up.

"It's Bree," I said.

Chavez quickly moved to the table. He motioned to Parker. Parker moved to a briefcase full of electronics, switches, and blinking lights that sat on the kitchen counter. Wires ran from the brief case to a lap top. On the lap top screen was a map. He put on a pair of headphones that were connected to the case. Chavez pointed at me.

"Keep him on the phone as long as possible," he said.

I answered. "Hello?"

"I'm sure they are tracing this call … or whatever it is they do nowadays, so I'll make this quick." I detested the smugness in Mason's voice. "Remove whatever it is they probably have hooked up to your cell phone and I'll call you back on another line later. And Jake, I'll be long gone by the time they get here, so tell them not to bother," Mason quickly hung up.

I put the phone back on the table.

"Get anything?" Merle asked.

Parker didn't answer.

"Parker, did yo—"

Parker silenced Merle with the raising of his index finger. Lint, Chavez, Merle, and I all stood quietly. Parker removed his headphones and began typing on the laptop's key board. We sat quietly waiting. His index finger glided across the touchpad moving the cursor from place to place.

Parker stared at the screen and said, "Mason's in the town of Conway, between Sherwood Drive and," he paused. "…Wright Boulevard. Between Mill Pond Road and Ninth Avenue."

"Lint, put in a call the Conway Police and then take a uniform and get out there. I'll contact the State Police," Merle said.

I sat back down at the table and put my head in my hands. *We'll get her back, Jake.*

Chapter Thirty-One

For the next few hours we heard a lot of chatter over the radio. The Conway Police Department, as well as the State Police, and Sheriff's Department were assisting us in the search for Bree.

It was a little after five by the time Lint got back to my house. We knew the story before he got there but he filled us in anyway. The search had been quickly narrowed down to a small area around the Coastal Mall Shopping Center in Conway. Officers checked cars, set up roadblocks, and went from store to store asking questions. Of course no one had seen anything. After an hour Bree's phone was found, smashed, in the mall parking lot. The phone was our only way to locate Mason.

I picked up my cell phone and removed the back. I then removed the small wire and memory chip that Chavez had installed and stuck it in my pocket. I put the battery back in and slid the back cover into place with a snap and put my phone in my pocket. I got up and made myself another cup of coffee.

An hour later my cell phone rang. Everyone sprang to their positions. Merle at my side, Chavez and Parker at the laptop. Lint was taking a shit.

"Hello?" I said.

"Hello, Jake. I trust you unhooked anything from your phone that might let anyone listen in," Mason said.

"I'm not getting anything," Parker whispered.

Chavez began typing on the laptop. "Merle, we're not getting a signal," he whispered.

"I did," I replied.

Merle's eyes went from me to Chavez and back.

"Jake, I want you to take the Conway Bypass to the 501. I want you to drive for sixteen miles, then take a left on to Grady Road, then a quick right on to Epson. Pull into the driveway of the first house you come to. And Jake, if anyone other than you pulls into this driveway, I'll put a bullet right through your wife's head. If you're not here by six-thirty, I'll put a bullet right through your wife's head. You understand?"

Parker and Chavez were still checking connections on the laptop when I told Mason I understood and hung up.

"*Dammit!*" Chavez said.

I pulled the wire and chip from my pocket and tossed it to Chavez.

"Goddammit, Jake," Merle said. "What did he say?"

"He said he would call back in the morning with instructions."

Lint came walking down the hall. "Phew! I wouldn't go in there for quite a while," he said, fanning the air with a rolled-up magazine before he took a seat at the table. He looked at his watch. "I wonder when this a-hole is gonna call?"

"He just called," Parker said.

"Why didn't someone yell to me?" Lint asked.

"You were doing some of your best police work," I said. "We didn't want to bother you."

"Oh, funny, Jake. Your police ... work ... isn't," Lint turned and walked away.

"Good one," I said.

I walked to the cupboard where we kept the to-go menus and took out the one for Domino's. "Pizza?" I asked.

"Hell, yeah!" came Lint's voice from the living room.

Merle rolled his eyes.

I walked over to the house phone that hung on the wall next to the refrigerator and pulled it from its cradle. I ordered three large pizzas with everything on them.

The words, "I don't like peppers and onions" quickly shot from Lint's gaping pork-trap.

"Two pizzas with everything on them and one large with just cheese and pepperoni." I gave the phone jockey my address and told them to deliver the pizzas on the Twenty-Fifth Avenue side of the house that I would open the garage door, and the delivery guy could walk in through the garage.

The phone jockey told me it would be around thirty-five minutes, thanked me, and hung up.

I looked out the window. At least a dozen uniforms were outside my house, keeping back the growing crowd. There were now three news vans, each with its own flood light. *Jesus, it's bright out there.*

Merle sent Parker out to let the uniforms know to let in the pizza delivery guy.

I joined Lint in the living room. He was sitting in my recliner. He had his shoes off and was grinding his smelly feet into the foot rest. *God, I hate him.*

"You got a soda or something, Jake?" Lint asked.

I sat on the couch. "Yeah, in the fridge. Help yourself."

"Uh, maybe I'll just wait till the pizza gets here." He leaned back, yawned and clasped his fingers behind his head.

"Yeah, you do that."

By the time the pizza arrived I had joined Merle, Parker, and Chavez at the kitchen table. We were playing cards, dealer's choice. I saw the headlights of the delivery truck and got up to push the garage door remote that we kept on the kitchen window sill. A few seconds later the delivery boy walked through the garage entrance into the kitchen with the pizzas in a warming bag. He took the three boxes out and set them on the table.

A mop of lank, greasy hair stuck out from under the delivery boy's sweat stained Domino's cap. He was about my size, but he had a pizza belly the size of a Volkswagen Beetle. It was easy to see what he found most desirable about working for a pizza company. Not the spiffiest representative the company had, but the kid intrigued me as I sized him up.

"Like, what's going on here? There's, like, cameras *everywhere*," the pimply faced boy said.

"We're shooting a porn. We were just waiting for the pizza delivery boy to arrive," Chavez said.

We were all shocked to hear Chavez say something funny. The pizza boy's eyes goggled. I thought he would shit his pants.

"He's *joking*," I said.

"For the first time ever," Merle added.

I pulled my money clip from my pocket and paid the boy what he had asked for. He turned and left.

I picked up the pizzas and brought them to the kitchen counter. I pressed the button to close the garage door. "Oh shit," I said. "I didn't tip the kid." I quickly went out the garage door.

The delivery boy was just getting into his delivery truck, tricked out with mega Domino's signage. "The garage door closed before I got out," he said.

"Yeah, two things," I said. "One, I forgot to tip you, and two, take off your hat and your shirt."

Chapter Thirty-Two

As I drove along 501 in my new pizza delivery truck, sporting my new shirt and hat, I wondered if anyone had gone to the garage yet. I knew Lint was probably stuffing his giant blow hole with pizza. I knew that he probably didn't grab a napkin and that grease was, at that moment, running down his fat, hairy arms and dripping onto my recliner. There was probably grease all over the television remote control, too. But I figured Merle and the others were smart enough to look in the garage. I imagined the hell that had broken loose.

I didn't tie up the poor boy or gag him or anything. I just simply and quickly explained the situation to him and asked him nicely if he would please just sit there in the garage until someone came for him. Of course, I was holding my gun the entire time I explained it to him. I wasn't pointing it at him, I was pointing it at the ground. He quickly agreed that my plan was a good one and gave me his shirt and hat. the polo shirt was half a size too big for me and smelled of pepperoni, and the hat had enough hair and pizza grease on it to lube my truck, but they would do.

I looked at my watch. It was 6:10 when I took a right off of 501 on to Grady Road. Mr. *Punctual, that's me.* Instead of taking a right on to Epson Road, I took a quick left into an old driveway that didn't look to me like it was in use anymore. I parked the truck behind some bushes and grabbed the binoculars sitting on the seat beside me that I had taken from the garage. There was a large tree and some bushes between me and the front of the house Mason had described. I could see the front door and the windows in the front of the house. I hoped no one could see me. I moved the binoculars from window to window. At one point I thought I saw someone pass in front of one of the windows, but it could have been my imagination.

I looked at the sky. It was too light out for me to go running across an open field without risking being spotted. The sun wouldn't be setting for another two hours or so and I didn't have that much time.

I restarted the truck and pulled back out onto Grady Road, drove back up to 501 and took a left. I drove about a hundred yards or so and took a left onto a tiny dirt road just barely big enough for one car. I slowly drove along. When I got to the end of the road I pulled the truck into the trees. I was now directly in back of the house.

I got out of the truck and took another look through the binoculars. Between the house and me were some pine trees, the driveway of another home, and then about fifty feet of open yard.

I stood in the pine grove watching the house. I thought of Mason standing in the woods, watching Helen Gere and Sam Chandler. He stood there silently, knowing that he was about to kill, just as I stood here now, knowing the same. I looked at my watch again. Six twenty-eight.

I tossed the binoculars back through the window and onto the seat. I lifted the side of my overlarge and fragrant Domino's shirt and removed my gun from its holster. I stooped over and, as quickly and, quietly as I could, made my way through the trees and across the driveway to another stout pine. I stood with my back to the tree. I peeked around the trunk at the house, and then quickly moved my head back out of sight.

I stood with the back of my head pressed against the rough bark of the pine. In the distance I heard a dog bark. I felt a bead of sweat run down my rib cage to the waist line of my pants. My heart was pounding. I took a deep breath and took off running to the corner of the house. When I got there I dropped to my knees and waited for a few seconds. There was no sound, no movement, no shots fired.

I slowly got to my feet and looked in the window above me. There were two people lying on the floor, a man and a woman. Their hands and feet were bound with duct tape and each had duct tape across their mouths. I stared at their chests. I couldn't tell if there was any movement.

I slowly made my way around the house and looked in each window. When I got to the fourth window and looked in to what must have been the living room, I could see Bree. She was sitting on the floor in the corner of the room. Her hands and feet were duct-taped together to keep her in the sitting position; her mouth was duct-taped, too. Duct tape, 1001 motherfucking uses.

Her eyes were open. She was looking around the room. Our eyes met. Her eyes widened. She hopped toward the window but fell over on her side. She stretched her neck to see me. I could hear her trying to scream from behind the duct tape. I put my finger to my lips to try and quiet her down but she kept struggling to get to me.

I heard the crunch of dry grass behind me. Everything flashed white and then darkness.

Chapter Thirty-Three

The next time I opened my eyes I was staring into my own lap. I raised my head. There was a sharp pain in my neck and the back of my head hurt. My vision was blurry. I wanted to rub my eyes but my arms wouldn't move.

I was sitting in a wooden chair in the middle of the room I had last looked in from the window. It was dark now. Light was coming from somewhere behind me, a hallway or bedroom perhaps. I couldn't turn my head far enough to see. I thought about calling out, but then thought it was best that no one knew I was awake.

My hands were tied behind me at the wrists and duct tape had been wrapped around my chest several times binding me to the back of the chair. Another chair similar to the one I was in sat empty facing me at the far wall. I sat quietly.

After a few minutes I heard movement behind me and the light above my head turned on. The light hurt my eyes.

"Shit, Jake, for a minute there I thought I had killed you," Mason said as he walked by my chair, leading Bree to the other chair. "Hit you a little too hard I guess. You must have one hell of a headache."

I said nothing. Bree was crying. Her shoulders shook. Muffled words came from behind the duct tape across her mouth. I think she said "I love you," but I couldn't be sure.

"There's probably aspirin over there in the cupboard, help yourself," Mason chuckled.

As Mason sat Bree in the chair I could see my gun tucked into his waistband.

I was still having trouble focusing my eyes. Mason was right, I did have one hell of a headache. I closed my eyes for just a second. Mason slapped me across the face as hard as he could. My ears rang.

"Wake up, Jake! I don't want you to die on me, for Chrissake." Mason grabbed my shoulders and shook me. I glared at him through my fog. "You gotta be awake to watch the show. Then you have to live a long healthy life remembering what happened here today knowing that you caused it all."

Mason left the room. Then I could hear him grunting. He was dragging something. It was the young woman from the first window. He dragged her to the adjacent wall and propped her up against it.

"Witnesses," Mason said to me. He left the room again and returned dragging the young man. He propped him up next to the woman.

The woman and man were both in their late twenties, early thirties. She had red hair and a face full of freckles. He had shoulder-length brown hair. She was dressed in pajamas. He had on sweats and no shirt. It was obvious, based on the way they were dressed, that Mason had broken in to their home while they were asleep.

Other than a small bruise under the young man's left eye, they appeared to be unharmed. They didn't look as scared as they should. Mason must have assured them that they wouldn't be harmed if they cooperated.

Mason left the room a third time, but this time he went to the kitchen.

"Jake," he called out from the kitchen. "Why do they always use three names?"

I said nothing.

"Unless you want another lump on your head you may want to join in the conversation."

"I don't know what you're talking about," I replied.

"You know, three names. On the news… they called me Phillip Allen Mason. Why do they do that?" Mason asked.

"I have no idea," I responded.

"John Wayne Gacy, Theodore Robert Bundy, Jeffery Lionel Dahmer, Phillip Allen Mason," he chuckled.

"Sounds about right," I said.

Mason laughed out loud again, a braying sound that set my teeth on edge. "Well, I'm not going to have sex with anyone after they're dead, and I sure as hell ain't going to eat anybody."

"Nice to know," I mumbled.

Mason returned with what he had gone for, a large butcher knife.

"Yeah, I wouldn't do any of that shit. That's just disgusting." He brandished the knife theatrically, swishing it through the air. "I'm just going to drag this knife across your wife's throat, and while she is gurgling and gasping for air, and choking on her own blood, I'm going to shoot her in the side of the head. She'll go out just like my family... and your partner, and that green young cop, and that old bitch and her daughter. I saw on the news that they still haven't found her. In New York they find someone dead in a dumpster almost every day, but somehow they missed her."

I said nothing.

"You're wondering why I killed Gere's daughter," Mason said.

"I figured it was just because you were a psychopath."

Mason laughed. "No, Jake. You see I spent almost eight years in that hospital. Therapy every day. Medication every day. I was really making progress, they said. I hadn't thought about you in years. Then one day I walk into the nurse's office for my meds, and there you are. There was a picture of you and some old lady in a newspaper clipping. You had this stupid grin on your face like you were so proud of yourself.

"Something in my head just snapped. From that point on all I could think about was finding and killing you. I asked the nurse what the picture was from. She told me the whole story about her mother, the robbery. Said you were the cop that solved the crime. She played it up a lot bigger than it was, I'm sure. I asked her where it happened. 'North Myrtle Beach,' she said. I noted the name on her nurse's badge: Lorraine Gere.

"From that day on I kept a journal. I wrote every thought I had in it. Plotted out what I was going to do, how I was going to do it. Slowly, as the weeks and months passed, my plan changed from killing you, to making you suffer.

"By this time my doctors had seen me fit to grant me day passes and even weekend passes. One Friday afternoon I had planned to take a weekend pass. I went down and showered, got dressed, and went back to my room to pack my bag. When I walked in my room, there was that bitch of a nurse, Lorraine, reading my journal. I grabbed a fork off of my lunch tray and held it to her throat. I told her she was going to walk out of the hospital with me. She was going to smile and act as though everything was fine. I told her if she did everything I told her, I would let her live. I lied. We walked out the front door of the hospital and down the nearest alley. I shoved that fork so far into her throat that it came right out the back of her neck." Mason chuckled a little.

No one moved. No one made a sound. Mason walked over closer to Bree. She stared into my eyes. Her eyes were screaming, *Help me.*

"Please, Mason, you don't have to do this," I said.

"Wow, Jake I've heard that line in a lot of movies but I didn't think anyone really said it. You're right though. I don't *have* to do this. I *want* to do this. I've wanted to do this for a long time."

Bree was crying again, but there were no tears.

Mason looked to the young couple, and pointed at me. "I want you two to remember everything he says, everything he admits to. You're the only jurors in this trial."

"Trial?" I asked.

"Tell these people what you did to my family, Jake. Tell them how you killed my whole family."

"I didn't kill your family, Mason. Your wife killed your family… and then killed herself."

Mason bounded over to Bree and ran the knife swiftly across her upper arm. The cut was deep and blood flowed from the wound. She cried out.

"Goddammit, Mason, don't… don't!" I screamed.

"Tell them how you killed my daughter and then blamed it on me."

"It was an accident!" I yelled.

"But it was your fault, not mine." Mason had tears streaming from his eyes. He wiped them away. "Tell them." He pointed the knife at the couple. They flinched.

"It was an accident. I'm sorry!" I yelled. "I'm sorry!"

"You're sorry … I'm sorry too, Jake," he said quietly. His shoulders relaxed. The tightness in his face faded away. "I'm sorry too."

Mason pulled the gun from his waistband and walked slowly toward Bree. She struggled with all her strength. When he reached her I made my move.

I quickly stood up as straight as I could. Still bound to the chair I charged at Mason, hitting him in the solar plexus with my right shoulder. He gasped. He tried to block me with the hand holding the knife. We both stumbled to the floor with me on top of him. I felt the burning and instant wetness as the knife plunged into my side.

Mason dropped the gun, it slid across the floor. He let go of the knife and tried to turn and reach for the gun. With all of my strength I smashed my forehead into his face, and then again. He turned and I rolled off of him. The knife came loose and fell to the floor.

I sprang to my feet as Mason crawled to the gun. I ran backwards to the wall behind, colliding with it and breaking the chair into pieces. I pulled my hands free of the duct tape. Mason picked up the gun and pointed it at me. I picked up one of the broken chair legs and threw it. Mason fired while turning to block the chair leg. The bullet hit the floor in front of me.

I ran at Mason again. As I leapt he fired again. The bullet struck me in the right leg. I landed on him, sending us both back to the floor. He brought the gun up. I grabbed his wrist and pounded it against the floor. He let go.

The gun slid away. I crawled toward it. Mason grabbed me by the waist and stuck his thumb in the knife wound. I cried out. I grabbed the gun and rolled to my back. Mason was on his knees, straddling my legs. I fired three times into Mason's chest. He fell backwards to the floor.

I pulled my legs out from under Mason's lifeless body and crawled to Bree. I picked up the knife and cut the tape around her wrists. She pulled the tape off of her mouth and threw her arms around me. I fell backwards and my weight pulled her from the chair. She sat on the floor and slid her lap under my head.

"Do you have your cell phone?" Bree asked.

"No. It's on the kitchen table back home."

"The phone lines here are cut and Phil smashed his cell and theirs," Bree said pointing at the couple across the room.

"Hopefully someone heard the shots," I said.

Ignoring my pain, I crawled over and began to untie the hapless couple, leaving a blood track in my wake. Bree rushed over to assist.

"You can't stop being a cop for one second, can you?" she sighed.

When the young couple was freed, I laid my head back on Bree's lap. She rubbed my forehead and ran her fingers through my hair and told me she loved me. I was losing a lot of blood.

"Hey," I asked, staring up at her. "Can we start taking more showers together?"

"What's wrong with you?" she answered, but a big, loving smile bloomed on her face.

"Oh shit."

"What's the matter?"

"I just remembered, I have to be back to work tomorrow."

Chapter Thirty-Four

It was toward the end of July before I put my running shoes back on. By that time I had also put fifteen pounds back on. Bree had been running a few times a week and was in great shape. I told her I would give it a whirl if she promised to take it slow.

We walked out onto the driveway and Bree began to stretch. I began to watch. When she had enough of being gawked at, we walked down the driveway. Lying in the driveway in front of us was a newspaper. I stopped and looked at Bree.

"I ordered it for you. They started delivering it this morning," Bree said.

"Oh," I answered.

We ran down Hillside to Twenty-First and took a right. Then we took a left onto Ocean Boulevard. *Wow it's hot,* I thought.

"Wow, it's hot," Bree said.

"Uh-huh," I responded. I looked at my watch. Eleven-fifteen.

As we approached Seventeenth Avenue I slowed and began walking. Bree looked back and did the same.

"You okay?" she asked.

"I will be," I answered, and went in to Molly Darcy's for some whiskey wings … and a ginger-ale.

The End

Preview from Rodney Riesel's

Sleeping Dogs Lie

From the Tales of Dan Coast

Chapter One

It was a beautiful day. The kind of day one would compare to the word, *paradise*. Sunny, a few clouds dotting the sky, but the kinds of clouds that move across the sky slowly, never seeming to move in front of the sun. It was seventy five degrees, and a light breeze blew off the ocean rustling the palm trees. The clean salt air was refreshing. Gulls flew overhead, and cried out. An air horn blew in the distance. Waves crashed against the beach. It was like a dream, a memory.

A man and a woman stood in the front yard of a modest beach house, next to a sign that read, "For Sale." The home was a one-story bungalow, white with green shutters. The dormer in the front gave the illusion of a second story, but there was none.

A short gravel driveway led up to the house, and a pathway of the same material led from the driveway to the front steps. Sitting planted in the front yard were two palm trees and next to the road was a mailbox mounted on a post. On top of the mailbox were painted the numbers 632.

The front steps led to a porch, completely enclosed in a metal, slightly rusted screen.

The couple were holding hands and facing the front of the house. The woman was grinning at the joke the man had just told about a real estate agent and a farmer's daughter.

"That's bad," she said.

"I didn't write it," he responded.

"No, but you told it. That makes you just as bad as the guy who wrote it."

"Where the hell is she?" he asked, "We said three-thirty."

"She'll be here. Calm down, Boob."

They both turned toward the road as they heard a car pull up across the street. It was a shiny new Porsche, dark blue, with the top down. The car skidded to a stop half in the road and half on the neighbor's lawn.

"I think her commission is too high," he said to his wife.

"You drive a Porsche," she returned.

"I'm rich, bitch," he responded, laughing. She playfully kicked his shin.

A woman climbed out of the car, a Clorox-blonde woman. Deeply tanned, some sun with a lot of bed mixed in. She was not old, but probably too old for the pony-tail through the Marlin's ball cap she was sporting. She wore bright red lipstick, a shirt that appeared to be one size too small. The top two buttons purposely undone, probably after she left the house in the morning. She was not the most beautiful woman in the world, but it was a sure bet that her husband thought she was. Especially in the Daisy Duke shorts she was wearing this afternoon.

"I wonder if this is the real estate agent, or the farmer's daughter?" he speculated to his wife.

"Be nice," she warned.

"You must be the Coasts," the agent said, holding out her hand.

"Yes. I'm Alex, and this is Dan," Alex said, reaching out to accept the sales woman's hand.

"I'm Emily Dixon. Sorry I'm late. Did you have a look around the property?"

"Yes we did, it's beautiful. The palm trees, the view. It's just what we were looking for," Alex replied.

"Try not to sound so eager," Dan said to his wife. "I was going to try and offer them less."

"I don't think they would take any less, Mr. Coast." Emily said matter-of-factly.

"Well not now they wouldn't." he said, as he glared at his wife.

"Places like this are in big demand, and going pretty fast right now. This is a decision that won't wait, Mr. Coast…Mr. Coast…?"

*****

"Mr. Coast… Mr. Coast?" she asked, shaking his leg, "Are you awake?"

"Wha, what the Christ do you want?"

"Are you Dan Coast?" she asked.

Dan Coast lay face down in a hammock, his black tee shirt and tan cargo shorts wrinkled. Dan's long arms hung over the sides of the hammock, his knuckles touching the sand. Dan lay there staring through the net at an empty bottle that lay next to his Ray Ban sunglasses. Dos Manos, the bottle read. *Good God. Did I drink that, or did someone hit me in the head with it? There's no blood dripping into the sand, I guess I must have drank it.*

"Yeah, I'm Coast. What do you want?" he answered.

Coast slowly turned his head toward the voice, rubbing his eyes, his mind slowly transferring from dream to reality. His face had the slight imprint of the hammock netting. His blue eyes were blood shot from a long night of alcohol abuse, and around his eyes the crow's feet showed his age. Laugh lines some people call them, and that may be the way Dan's started out. In recent years however they were due to long nights, too much booze, and squinting at paradise's sun. Most days the lines on his face were not so prominent, but these rough nights made them more noticeable.

"Someone told me you could help me," she replied.

"Yeah, who?"

"He said he was a good friend of yours."

Well that narrowed it down to about six from an island of twenty three thousand. Coast didn't have a lot of friends. He had acquaintances. He had drinking buddies. He had people he worked for. He had people who worked for him. But he didn't consider any of them friends. Some of them probably considered him a friend, and that was fine with Dan. He had learned long ago that more good came from being liked, than it did from liking someone.

He pulled himself up out of the hammock with a groan. *Jesus Christ*, he thought, *you never heard Gilligan or Skipper bitch about their back, and they slept in a hammock every night.*

Dan stood by the hammock trying to subtly stretch different parts of his five foot, eleven inch body. First his neck, and back, then his wide shoulders and legs. If his uninvited guest didn't notice the stretching, she surely heard the cracking of bone. Dan's mentality and sense of humor may have still been that of a teenage boy, but the rest of him wasn't getting any younger. The creaking and cracking was a new language his body had learned in the last few years. Its way of telling him he was old. Too old to stay up drinking in a local bar all night, and definitely too old to sleep in a hammock all night. Dan heard what his body was telling him, and even thought it might believe it, but convincing Dan was going to take a few more years at least. Although Dan was beginning to feel the effects of aging in recent years, he was still in pretty good shape on the outside. He was in his mid-forties, but if he laid off the booze for a few days, he could easily pass for a man in his mid-thirties, but he didn't lay off the booze often. A slight belly had formed, but nothing he couldn't suck in and hold when the right woman strolled by, and most times that woman looked back and smiled. His hair was starting to turn grey, but he told himself it was turning grey in all the right spots. He told himself he looked distinguished. Dan's hair had thinned a little, but lately he was getting it cut shorter, thinking no one would notice.

"Help you how?" he asked.

"My friend is missing," she replied.

"Boyfriend?" Dan asked, already knowing the answer.

"Yes, boyfriend."

"Maybe he just got sick of you, and went back to the mainland. You know, that happens a lot down here. The girl thinks they are soul mates, the boy gets down here and sees what a woman is supposed to look like in a bikini, and he goes crazy. The women are a little younger, a little browner, and in a lot better shape. No offense."

"None taken," she responded in a not too convincing tone. "Go on."

"Sometimes he shacks up with one of these beauties for a few days and then comes back with his tail between his legs. Sometimes he's never seen again. Sometimes he just goes home," Dan finished.

"That's some speculation, Mr. Coast. You really know how to make a woman feel special." She said.

She was right, Dan was being a prick. A mood brought on by a lousy night's sleep, too much alcohol, and being shot down in front of a bar full of people by a twenty-four year old stewardess. A stewardess that seemed pretty interested earlier in the night but lost most of that intrigue as Dan grew drunker, louder, and more obnoxious as the evening progressed. Dan could be charming when sober, but sometimes he took a turn in the other direction when drunk. Now Dan was taking his anger and frustrations out on this woman, a woman who came to ask him for help. She just seemed to remind Dan a little too much of last night's stewardess. This woman too had blonde hair, she was tall, thin. It was obvious she took good care of herself, exercised, ate right. She also had that same tone of voice as the stewardess. That way of speaking and moving that let you know she was just a little bit smarter than you, a little bit better. Dan didn't like people who acted like that, and he could feel himself not liking this woman very much.

"Hey, I'm just saying," Dan continued, "maybe he's not missing. Maybe he knows exactly where he is, and exactly what he wants, and maybe what he wants is to not be found."

"He wouldn't have left without me, and he sure wouldn't have left me for someone else. At least not yet," she said.

"I'm not so sure about that. I've known you for about five minutes and…ah never mind. How long has this guy been missing?" Dan asked, mustering as much sincerity as his sarcasm would allow.

"Since Wednesday, around two pm. We were lying by the pool. A hotel employee came out and told him there was a call for him at the front desk. He went in to answer it, and that's the last time I saw him." As she finished speaking she took a deep breath and moisture appeared at the corners of her eyes.

"So, to make a long story short, two days? When did you get here to the island?"

"Late Monday night," she explained. "We left Miami right after my husband's funeral."

"Like sands through the hour glass," he whispered to himself.

"What?" she snapped.

"Nothing. Listen, I'll see what I can do. I'm not going to guarantee that I'll find him, but I get paid either way. Up front and in cash. Is that going to be a problem?

"That won't be any problem at all, Mr. Coast," she replied.

"It's Dan. Meet me at Red's at three, it's a small bar on Charles Lake Road. I have a few more questions and we'll discuss the amount of the payment."

She agreed, thanked him, turned, and walked briskly away.

Dan didn't need the money. It's not that he already had too much; he just didn't need any more. His winnings got him everything he wanted. Well, almost everything. He still had neighbors who bugged him, they still borrowed things, their dogs still barked at night. It's just now his neighbors were a little browner, a little less clothed, and they never needed to borrow his snow shovel. Even though he didn't need the money, he still liked to get paid. He tried living off his winnings when he first arrived, fishing, lying on the beach, drinking, but that got old real fast. All but the drinking, that is.

Dan had been self-employed in his old life back on the mainland. Just like his father before him, he was a carpenter, mostly doing home improvements and remodeling jobs. He was used to working hard, and he was used to getting paid. Some habits died hard.

He watched as she walked across the yard, hips swaying, and up the gravel pathway toward the front of his house. Now that his head had started to clear a little from the tequila fog, he noticed how good she looked, and why she had had one too many men in her life. *Wow, she looks good from behind, not too bad from the front either. It's funny though, how annoying can turn a 10 into a 7. Crap, what was her name?*

Dan started to call out to her. *What should I call out?* he wondered, *Ma'am, Miss, Hey, annoying lady? Ah forget it. I'll see her at Red's later anyway. Then she'll tell me her name. And if she doesn't show up, then it doesn't matter anyhow.*

He rubbed his eyes, his head, and stretched his arms toward the tops of the palm trees. He bent over and touched his toes. Then stood back up straight and cracked his neck from side to side. With a heavy drop he sat back down, laid back, and gazed up at the tops of the palm trees.

That was a tough workout, I'm going to need a little power nap.

Coast closed his eyes. He wasn't used to being woken up this early after a long night out. It had been a long time since there had been someone to wake him up, and even longer since there was a good reason to be up. After moving to the island, Dan's motto had pretty much become, "If God wanted everything done now, he wouldn't have put so many numbers on the clock."

ALSO BY RODNEY RIESEL

Sleeping Dogs Lie

From the Tales of Dan Coast

A mystery set in the Florida Keys follows Dan Coast, an unlicensed private detective of sorts, as he is hired to find the missing boyfriend of a woman who herself soon ends up missing. When someone from the woman's past unexpectedly shows up at Dan's home, with a story of faked deaths and missing life insurance money; Dan along with his sidekick Red set out to find the money, and the woman.

ISBN: 978-0-9883503-0-4

Ocean Floors

From the Tales of Dan Coast

The second installment in the Dan Coast series, Ocean Floors, is a tale of mystery and possible romance when a chance meeting with a beautiful young woman leads Dan and his trusted sidekick Red down a road of murder and kidnapping. Join Dan and Red as they try to solve the murder while searching for a missing friend.

ISBN: 978-0-9894877-0-2

Impaled

An Adirondack Short Story

Eric Stone is an investigator with The Town of Webb Police Department. Chuck Little is Head Ranger at the Nick's Lake campground. An unlikely duo, together they work to solve a murder that mimics a spree of gruesome murders taking place years earlier. Is it a copycat, or has the murderer resurfaced after all of these years? Join Stone and Little as they piece together the clues to solve this mystery taking place in the small village of Old Forge in the Adirondack Mountains.

North Murder Beach

A Jake Stellar Novel

The first installment of the story of North Myrtle Beach police detective, Jake Stellar. The spring bike rallies have ended, the spring breakers have all gone back to school, and the summer tourist season is a few weeks away. What better time for a police officer to take a nice quiet relaxing week off from work? That's what Jake Stellar had in mind. That is until someone from his past resurfaces to remind him of a terrible secret he has spent years trying to forget. In North Murder Beach, a story of revenge, Jake is unwillingly and violently forced to confront his secret from his past.

ISBN: 978-0-9894877-1-9

The Coast of Christmas Past

From the Tales of Dan Coast

Coast of Christmas Past is the third book in the Dan Coast series of books. Dan Coast is all set to spend Christmas just the same way he has every year for the past few years; alone and drunk. But when uninvited, unexpected guests arrive and throw a wrench into his holiday plans he is forced to sober up (slightly), and throw on a smile. Just when it seems nothing else could go wrong, a close friend is injured in what appears, to the police, to be a drug deal gone bad. Dan Coast and his sidekick, Red jump into action to find the truth while their friend lies unconscious in the hospital.

ISBN: 978-0-9894877-3-3

The Man in Room Number Four

When a mysterious stranger arrives in the small coastal town of Dunquin Cove, Maine it appears as though Claire and her young son, Mica's prayers have been answer.

But who is he, and why is he really here? Join Claire and her guests at the Colsome House Bed and Breakfast as they piece together the mystery of the Man in Room Number Four.

ISBN: 978-0-9894877-2-6

Ship of Fools

From the Tales of Dan Coast

Ship of Fools is the fourth book in The Tales of Dan Coast series and begins where Coasts of Christmas Past left off. Find out how Dan deals with the death of a young friend, while looking into the disappearance of a new friend's sister. Join Dan, Red, and Skip as they fumble their way through a new mystery.

ISBN: 978-0-9894877-4-0

Beach Shoot

A Jake Stellar Series

It's a beautiful Sunday morning in North Myrtle Beach and Emily Bowen, a wife and mother of four, lies dying on the beach. Jake Stellar returns in Beach Shoot, a new mystery by Rodney Riesel.

Beach Shoot is the second Jake Stellar book and sequel to the Amazon Best Seller North Murder Beach. In Beach Shoot, Jake finds himself teamed up with the most unlikely of partners, his nemesis and fellow detective Avis Lint. Join Jake and Avis as they piece together the clues in this thrilling new mystery.

ISBN: 978-0-9894877-5-7